A CUP OF REVENGE

Noble Press

A CUP OF REVENGE

A Drew Davies Railway Mystery – Book 2

Gail Noble-Sanderson

Published by Noble Press, LLC
Mt. Vernon, Washington
gnoble_sanderson@comcast.net
gailnoblesanderson.com

Editing by Spellbinder Editorial
Cover Art by Kathleen Noble
Cover design and typesetting by Enterline Design Services
Author photo by John Anderson Photography

ISBN 978-0-9991386-8-7(paperback) / ISBN 978-0-9991386-9-4 (e-book)
Library of Congress Control Number: pending

Printed in the United States of America

ALSO BY GAIL NOBLE-SANDERSON

A Drew Davies Railway Mystery
The Book of Rules — Book 1

The Lavender Meuse Series
The Lavender House in Meuse
The Passage Home to Meuse
The Lavender Bees of Meuse

Women's Work

The front door closed and locked
the children in the window watch
neighbors walking down the street,
those ladies in their heels and hats.
The men have left, by foot or bus
to work in town, one speeds past
on his bicycle. It's after nine.
Mothers, elbow-deep in water,
suds, their bundled headscarves
wrapped and knotted on the top,
dark cotton dresses to their calves,
will soon hang washing on the line,
now no one's watching as they ply
the secrets of their domesticity.

Linda Conroy – Poet

This book is dedicated to my remarkable sister and brother,

Kathleen Annette Noble, PhD

and

Dr. William Howard Noble

TABLE OF CONTENTS

A NOTE FROM THE AUTHOR

Historical fiction is the writing genre with benefits: benefits for both the reader and the author. Gathering accurate and relevant research is the foundation for writing our stories. And while authors can mine the many trusted sites available on the web, in books, and in journal articles, there is no better way to ground your writing than experiencing history firsthand.

Seated at our desks in front of computers, we conduct online research and read many tomes of knowledge about the time and place of our stories. We accumulate all we can to educate us as to how the peoples of our story lived. Then we can take one final step. We book a journey, pack a bag, and go to that place. And for even just a little while, we get to live our story.

That is when research comes alive and allows the storyteller to give readers a firsthand account of what laverbread in Mumbles actually tastes like on the tongue, what feelings are evoked as you stand before a 2000-year-old cathedral built on Roman ruins, what insights can strengthen your telling of a story after interviewing a World War II veteran, becoming friends with Welsh historians as they take you to castles and churches, or standing among the 13,000 crosses at the Verdun, France, battlefield cemetery. The author's experiences in live research enhance their characters' lives. History comes alive when the writer is there, living in the places and witnessing what they write about.

As my husband and I walked along the River Meuse in Eastern France some years ago, he came across something nudging against his shoe. He bent over and dusted off what was lying beneath the dirt and found a very large and rusted key. This key would be similar to the one that opened my character Marie's home. Her house would have stood somewhere along those banks in 1919. When my husband presented me with this key, I was quite overcome, so very grateful for the experience of having my story become real.

This last September, as we stood along the beautiful balustrade at the boardwalk on the pier in Mumbles Village, the venerable old lighthouse standing sentry in the Bristol Sea, I knew many of my characters would find themselves doing the same in the book you are now holding in your hands.

I so hope our travels to Wales and the experiences we had there, as I continued my research for these Drew Davies Railway Mysteries, will help bring these stories to life for you, the reader. It is only through the truths of history that we recognize and fight for the truths of our future.

PROLOGUE

The Arrival – Friday, March 14, 1947

The sun hung low in the late afternoon sky. Drew Davies could hear the train nearing the depot as she stepped onto the platform. To her right, she saw the small group of parishioners clustered together, waiting to welcome their new vicar. She raised her hand in greeting as they momentarily glanced her way. Some smiled in acknowledgment, but most kept their eyes focused on the train slowly making its entrance into the Swansea, Wales, station. Drew could sense the anticipation and perhaps even hesitation of those waiting, not knowing what to expect of their new vicar, Liam O'Neill.

Liam stood on the metal platforms between the cars as the train rumbled into the station, the moving plates gliding over and under one another. Suddenly, the train jerked forward as the screech of braking wheels filled the air. He quickly grabbed the metal handlebar with his left hand, reaching down with the other to take hold of the leather straps of his duffle bag.

Stepping closer to the open window, he could see a small gathering on the platform. He knew this contingent of well-intentioned people were here to welcome their new vicar. He wondered, not for the first time, if he were making a terrible mistake.

CHAPTER 1

MARA'S CALL – FRIDAY EVENING, FEBRUARY 28

Drew hurried from the kitchen to answer the insistent ringing of the telephone on the corner table in the alcove beside her bedroom.

"Davies residence. This is Drew."

"Oh, how fortunate you answered my call. I didn't think anyone was at home, it rang so long. Saves us both time, you know. I'm ringing to say that the new vicar will be arriving in two weeks' time, on the fourteenth. The men of the church have done a great deal to put the house in order, taking down the false wall and completely painting the first floor. And we women have stripped and polished the wood floors to gleaming. So now we need to put our minds to the gardens, and that is where we can use your help.

"I have heard on more than one occasion that you and your grandmother are excellent gardeners, and your vegetable and flower beds are organized and prolific. Getting to the point, as I really do need to go, we would like to hire you to weed, prepare, and plant all the garden beds of the vicarage. None of us are young and strong, so this lies to you, Miss Davies.

"Therefore, I will meet you tomorrow morning at nine o'clock and show you what requires your attention. Of course, we will pay you, in addition to cleaning and preparing the house that also needs to be done before the new man arrives.

"But I must go now, Miss Davies. Therefore, I will see you on Saturday. I really do *not* have the time for chit-chat."

The line clicked off and Drew stood with the receiver in hand, her ear ringing, realizing she had not actually been asked if she would do this garden work but rather commanded. But that was how Mara Roberts, president of the Women's Church Auxiliary of the Anglican Church in Mumbles, ran her life and the lives of others, directing and recruiting, never entertaining the notion that people had other commitments and responsibilities. And maybe, just maybe they did not want to do her bidding. Drew wondered if anyone ever refused their marching orders.

Although Mara's assuming phone call could have perturbed her, in truth, the tangled gardens of dead vines and mounds of weeds had tormented Drew since the day she began the cleaning and meal preparation for the former vicar. She was quite looking forward to tomorrow's work and began quickly compiling a list in her head of garden implements to take with her. Perhaps Granda would let her borrow his lorry.

"That was a rather short, one-sided conversation, Drew. Whoever was it?" asked Naomi.

"That was Mara, informing me I have been recruited to clean up the gardens at the vicarage before the new man arrives, which is in two weeks' time," Drew answered, sitting down to dinner with her granda, Howard, and her nonna, Naomi.

Nonna passed Drew the platter of spaghetti alla puttanesca, saying, "Is that enough time to get that all done? Sounds like a big task and many hours after work, at that."

"I am very much looking forward to getting my hands in those gardens, and I can work on Saturdays and Sundays. Mara says they have been working inside the house, too."

"Did she say what they did?" asked Granda.

As Drew related all that Mara had said, she couldn't help but remember that just five short months ago she had gone to clean the vicarage and found Vicar

Hughes in his bed—murdered with a large knife. Drew, with the help of Granda, had solved the murder, and the murderer was now in prison. The villagers of Mumbles were eager to put those events in the past and looked forward to the arrival of their new clergyman.

"May I take some of our garden tools with me, Granda? And the lorry as well? After I meet Mara, I'm going to stay and begin attacking the gardens. She also said I was to finish preparing the house. I'm hoping all this extra work will result in a tidy sum of hard-earned money," Drew said, tucking into her breakfast. She was always hungry and often wondered if, once the many years of post-war rationing ended, she would ever feel full again.

Drew held a clerical position in the railway station in Swansea, where her grandfather, Howard, was station master and dispatcher. She had her sights on a new position that would have her working directly with the engines and trains, her dream job. She hadn't yet told Granda, but she was going to apply for the position of passenger van guard and was waiting for the right time. The position wasn't posted as yet, but she knew it would be opening up in the next month or so. And she would be ready.

CHAPTER 2

A MEETING AT THE VICARAGE – SATURDAY, MARCH 1

Saturday morning found Drew in the shed, sorting through garden implements to load into the lorry. She was quite eager to attack those unholy gardens. Into the truck went the long-handled clippers, pruning shears, rake, shovel, small trowel, knife, two pails, and her gardening gloves. She thought about hauling the wheelbarrow into the lorry but decided not to, as Granda had made it clear that Mara's battalion of church helpers needed to do their share of the work.

"You clear the gardens' refuse into piles, and they can haul it all away," were his exact words.

Drew was first to arrive at the vicarage, which gave her time to unload the lorry and walk the overgrown beds lining the inside of the property's fence before Mara made her entrance. Drew still had her key to the house and was eager to see how the inside looked, now that they had painted and removed the false wall that had hidden the staircase. But she knew she did not dare go into the vicarage without Mara. She wondered if any of the tired old furniture in the parlor had been replaced with pieces less reminiscent of the ugly events that occurred there. She certainly hoped so.

Prompt as always, Mara arrived precisely at nine o'clock, talking to Drew before she had even gotten out of her car. Drew missed the first half of what she said but knew there was no reason to say so. It would be repeated, probably three additional times.

". . . and, of course, you must rake all the branches, sticks, and such into tightly formed piles, and some of the men will come haul them away. I do hope you have brought what you need. Oh—" Mara paused as she noticed Drew's assortment of tools lying on the ground. "I see you did indeed come to work, and that is to be commended."

"Of course, Mrs. Roberts. I have already looked at all the gardens and have a plan. Today, I want to begin removing all that is dead and overgrown. I will start here at the front, clearing the beds on both sides of the fence, then work my way round to the back. I'll return tomorrow and continue. It looks as though it will take about four to five days to clear it all. I'll do most of the work on the weekends and then evenings after work, as needed. I hope to have it all prepped for planting before the vicar arrives."

"Excellent! I do like a young person willing to work hard. Just keep track of your time. Now, come inside the house, and I can show you what needs to be done there."

Drew brushed her hands on her work trousers and followed the well-dressed woman to the front door. She admired the older woman's sense of style, and despite years of mending and repair to everyone's clothing, Mrs. Roberts always looked smart. This morning, she wore a pale green dress of thin wool and a matching jacket with large gold buttons. She looked as though she were on her way to a formal luncheon. Drew thought she probably did not, nor ever would, own a pair of trousers. On the other hand, Drew wished to wear nothing *but* the comfortably loose pants.

Entering the house, her eyes went immediately to the small parlor on the right. Drew was disappointed to find that, while the furniture had indeed been replaced, it was as dreary as what had been there before. And worst of all, there were awful white throw pillows embroidered with a profusion of blue cornflowers on a very ugly dark purple sofa. Two mismatched, overstuffed brown chairs sat in front of the hearth, one on each side of the very clean and very cold fireplace. The square wooden table with its small lamp and telephone, the same one from which Drew had rung the police after finding the murdered vicar, still stood sentry beside the bereft sofa.

She wondered if the new vicar would find the room as depressing as she did. Perhaps, if he was an aged man, he might find it familiar and somehow soothing. But the vicar was said to be young and hopefully a person that cared at least a little about aesthetics.

"Doesn't this parlor look lovely, Miss Davies? The ladies really outdid themselves. As you know, there is so little to be found in these times, but I think we managed very well," Mara said with a short nod. "And the glorious floors add a luster to it all, don't they?"

"I'm sure the new vicar will very much appreciate all the work that has been done on his behalf. Where did you say you had put the clean bed linens?"

"Well, on the beds of course, and there are two bedrooms now. The new man, for whatever reason, has decided he wants to have his bedroom and personal study up on the first floor, in that large room. And he has made this decision sight unseen, mind you. Seems rather rash, but it certainly isn't for me to say."

"Might I go up and have a look and see what I'll be needing to do?"

"Yes, of course, but you won't find much. Just the bed we found for him and the desk that was already up there. The clean linens, drapes, and bed sheets are in both bedrooms, and the soaps, rags, mop, and bucket are still in the pantry where they were left. I think you will have everything you need. If not, do buy it or find second-hand goods and you will be reimbursed. Be sure you have the receipts, of course."

Drew climbed the stairs, now exposed after the false wall hiding access to Vicar Hughes's secrets had been removed. The heavy wooden banister still needed a polish, but the stairs were gleaming. Drew would shine the banister when she did the final cleaning before the vicar arrived.

It was odd entering this upper room from the stair landing, as the other two times she had been here she entered from inside the pantry, climbing a secret ladder made of shelves. No one but the vicar and his sister, and possibly whoever he was working with, knew this secret room had existed. And now it was to be the new vicar's bedroom. The view from the windows was expansive, the best view in the cottage. One could see far south out to the Bristol Sea and east almost to Swansea. It even had a wardrobe and a cozy fireplace. What a wonderful bedroom and study.

"Alright, Drew, let's get moving, as I need to be on my way now," Mara called up the stairs. "No time to dilly-dally."

Drew hurried back down at Mara's loud beckoning and looked quickly to the left into the bathroom and other two rooms.

"I see the bed that was in Vicar Hughes's room and the desk that was in his study. Will those stay?"

"Yes. The new vicar requested one of the rooms remain as a bedroom where guests could sleep, and the other will become his pastoral office where he will meet with parishioners. I assure you the bed has been replaced, but we saw no reason to change out the chair and desk in the office."

"Now, one last thing, Miss Davies. Let us step into the kitchen. You are to do a deep cleaning in both the kitchen and the bathroom, including wiping down every surface and inside the cupboards and, of course, the dishes, pots, pans, eating utensils, serveware, the larder, cookstove, and oven. I assume you did that from time to time for Vicar Hughes, as things were always so tidy and clean."

Drew nodded, but in fact, the former vicar seemed to so seldom eat what she prepared and never cooked for himself that nothing ever required a "deep cleaning." But she would do as requested. It would all be in good order when this vicar took possession of his new residence.

"Mrs. Roberts, can you please tell me what you know about the new vicar? Where he is from and how old he might be?"

"Well, I suppose," said Mara with a sniff, pulling on her gloves. "And then I really do need to leave. His name is Liam O'Neill, originally from Belfast and, as I understand, quite young for the position. But as is appropriate, he will be on a probationary period, so we will have time to see how it all works out. I must say, I was surprised when the church sent us such a young man, and one from Ireland, at that. But, of course, I was not consulted." With another sniff and a shrug, Mara bid Drew goodbye, saying over her shoulder as she stepped out the door, "I assume you still have your key?"

Drew nodded and took a deep breath as the door closed behind Mrs. Roberts.

It was now almost ten o'clock, and Drew worked steadily in the gardens until one, when her stomach rumbled. Standing up, she stretched her back and long legs, having knelt on the ground for the last three hours. She brushed herself off, removed her garden gloves, now caked with soil, and stood a moment, admiring the amount of work she had accomplished in such a short time.

She had started with the front beds to the left as you walked through the entry gate. They were now mostly cleared of the largest of the overgrowth. After lunch, she would clear the remainder and rake it all into piles—tightly raked piles, of course, she reminded herself with a smile.

She decided to eat inside at the familiar kitchen table. She set the kettle to boil and then scrubbed her hands and washed her face before walking through the house once again, this time at her leisure.

Looking though the kitchen windows to the back gardens, she thought, if she worked all the afternoon and tomorrow as well next Saturday and Sunday, she might be able to finish. If not, she would come directly from work the week before he arrived. She would also make up the beds and do a final cleaning in the house a few days before his appearance. Drew was tempted to make a platter of cookies and leave them on the kitchen table, but also knew that Mara and her auxiliary ladies would stock his pantry and larder to overflowing and prepare enough casseroles to see him through many meals. Smiling, she tidied the kitchen and went back to the gardens, where she worked until dusk.

CHAPTER 3

THE HONOURABLE GRACE DUVALL – WEDNESDAY, MARCH 5

Thursday found Sam and Drew eating lunch at her desk. "You're staying over in London again this weekend? Weren't you just at Pine Grove?"

Sam swept his fingers through his dark curls, always a sign of frustration, and nodded his head. "*Ie*, and again this week. Mother's closest childhood friend, Baroness Duvall, will be returning to England with her daughter, Grace. She and I grew up together and were reluctant playmates."

"Reluctant playmates? What does that mean?" said Drew, taking a large bite of her lunch.

"Every time the baroness came to visit with Mother, or we went to their home for a luncheon, I was dragged along and sternly told to 'play nicely' with Grace. This was, of course, before we were in school, but I remember well all the badgering that girl did to me, forcing me to play whatever games she wanted. If I refused, she threw a fit and kicked me hard in the knees, and if I complained, I would receive a threat from Mother. I couldn't wait till either they left our home or we left theirs."

Drew smiled. "A young bully, was she?"

"It isn't funny. She really was, and I've no desire to become 'reacquainted,' as Mother suggests.

"Where have they been living if not in England?"

"In Paris, for the last ten years. Having spent the war years there under the occupation, they are eager to return home to their estate. I understand it suffered quite a bit of damage during the blitz, and the baron has been in a mad rush trying to get it all repaired. They weren't supposed to return until the manor was put back together, but mother says Grace insisted they return to England immediately. My parents have invited them as houseguests until their home is ready. Which I hope is very soon, as I won't be going home again until they've left."

"That is very kind of your parents and very unkind of you, Samuel. I would expect nothing less from them and a little more graciousness from you. Will Grace have her own family there at Pine Grove as well?

"Grace?" Sam laughed and shook his head. "No, she isn't married. Mother says she just finished university and is focused on what she calls her 'career,' whatever that could be."

"Why did you laugh when you said she wasn't married?

"Mother always called Grace a 'wild child.' She spent more time climbing trees and swinging from branches than she did walking on the ground. She was spoiled, arrogant, and, as I said, mean. I cannot imagine anyone marrying such a horrible person."

"Well, people do grow up and change. When was the last time you saw her?"

"I was just heading to university, and she must have been about sixteen, still as unlikable as always and . . ." Sam paused mid-sentence and looked wide-eyed at Drew. "I have a great idea! You come with me this weekend. You know Mother would love to have you, and I need, really need your support. Claire and my nephews are coming to luncheon as well. You know it will be fun."

"*You* are a coward, Sam Provens! Afraid of a girl and in need of my protection. Well, I suppose I could accompany you, just to keep you safe from the 'wild child.'" Drew smiled and brushed crumbs from her trousers. Thinking she would work in the vicarage gardens after work today and tomorrow, and Friday, if needed, going to Pine Grove for the weekend would work out well.

"Right. It's settled. We'll leave Saturday morning on the early train. I'll be a passenger rather than the engine driver, so we can sit together. I'll ring today and let my parents know you'll be with me. As usual, I am sure Father will meet us at Paddington. Thank you, Drew! My family will be delighted, and I will be indebted."

Afraid she might change her mind, Sam jumped up from his chair, gathered his lunch scraps and cup, and bolted for the door. "I'll meet you on the platform. Bring a few of your nice things to wear. You know the ones I mean."

Drew smiled thoughtfully as she ate the last of her lunch and drank her cold tea. She was more than a little curious about Grace Duvall and could not help wondering about his mother's suggestion that the two childhood friends 'get reacquainted.' She was surprised at the twinge of what might be jealousy taunting her heart.

CHAPTER 4

LUNCHEON AT PINE GROVE – SATURDAY, MARCH 7

The sun shone through the large windows of spacious Pine Grove Manor, the elegant estate of Sam's parents, Douglas and Kathleen Provens.

Kathleen accompanied Drew to her usual room, plying her with questions about how Naomi and Howard were getting on. Drew had some time before lunch to change clothes and fix her hair, even adding some color to her cheeks and lips. Being here, in this beautiful family home, was always such a pleasure, and she found it familiar and comforting as she listened to the muted hum of people talking below.

As Drew entered the dining room, bright beams of sunlight pierced through sparkling windows, striking the cut-crystal chandelier hanging from the high ceiling. The candlesticks gracing the well-laid luncheon table cast brilliant prisms along the walls of the elegantly appointed room. Drew was mesmerized by the colors. It was as though the room had an aura of its own—positive and radiant.

Poppy, the Provens's cook, housekeeper, and family friend, had laid a feast upon the table. Drew knew that she was a favorite of Poppy's and saw that she had included some of Drew's favorite dishes. As Poppy placed deviled eggs, a basket of her homemade rolls, and a plate of butter in front of Drew, the cook leaned down and said, "Enjoy, Drew Girl. We are so glad you are here."

Her mouth was watering shamelessly. Drew didn't allow herself to wonder how they had acquired so much butter and so many eggs. Perhaps they now had a cow or two and some chickens on their many hectares of land.

The table was as familiar as her bedroom up on the first floor. She usually visited the Provens's once during every season of the year, and whichever season, she found herself at her own appointed place at the table. Neither Grace's father, the baron, nor Sam's father, Douglas, were present at lunch. Not surprising, as they would be at work in the City.

Kathleen, always dressed in understated elegance, sat smiling at her guests from one end of the table, and Baroness Duvall, quite lavishly attired in pink satin brocade, sat opposite her. Sam was to his mother's right and Grace opposite Sam. Drew sat, as was usual, beside Sam, and his sister Claire opposite her. Poppy often joined the family at meals, but since they had guests, today she tended the table. Drew would visit her later in the kitchen and insist on helping her with the dishes—which Poppy would soundly refuse.

Mrs. Provens motioned for the guests to serve themselves, and as people began passing bowls and platters of aspic, deviled eggs, cold salmon with fresh peas, asparagus, and a potato salad, Drew reached for a warm roll, pulled it apart, and heaped butter on each of its two halves. She also placed another roll on her plate. She was ravenous, as usual, and Poppy's rolls were unrivaled.

Light conversation ensued, those sitting beside one another and across remarking on the fine weather and the even finer lunch laid before them.

The baroness, in a tone of voice capturing everyone's attention, said, "Grace has one term of university to complete and then she is wanting to take up her career in banking. Isn't that correct, Grace darling?" The baroness smiled to the table at large.

"And what does that mean, Grace? I can hardly see you as a bank clerk," said Sam with a wry smile.

Grace looked at him with an expression somewhat opposite of the smile on her face and replied, "Actually, your father and I have had more than one conversation about a position at his bank, perhaps in the loan and investment department."

Grace might have been a precocious 'wild child' when young, but the woman Drew was now observing seemed serious to a fault. She was strikingly beautiful and utterly chic. Her blonde hair was coiled into a perfect chignon, and her small diamond earrings complemented her dress of blue wool, the color closely matching her long-lashed eyes. She wore no rings on her fingers. Drew clearly saw Grace's aura dancing around her in hues of green threaded with black. She exuded an intense, tightly controlled energy. Drew had never seen a lovelier nor more confident woman.

She also noticed the young woman took only very small portions of food onto her plate and then merely pushed the food around. What a waste and rather rude, thought Drew, and Grace did not even take a roll and butter. Drew decided to eat what would have been Grace's allotment of rolls and enjoyed every bite as she continued watching the conversation with growing interest.

"Well, good for you, Grace. I'm glad Father can perhaps find something suitable for you at the bank." Sam said this with a dismissive wave of his fork, a barbed salute to her good prospect.

"Clearly, you don't understand, Samuel. It isn't your father doing me a favor. It is rather about the skills and expertise I will undoubtedly bring to the bank. It's about looking ahead to the future and bringing younger minds into the fold. It *is* a new day, after all."

Grace finally took two small bites of lunch, then carefully placed her knife and fork side by side across the top of her plate and leaned across the table toward Sam. "And that leads me to another point, Samuel. Don't you think it is about time you grew up and assumed the mantle of your heritage and joined the firm as well? I was surprised when your mother told me you were still playing with trains. Really, it is quite reprehensible on your part to neglect your family's legacy."

Sam laughed out loud, causing Drew to choke on a forkful of peas. "If my father understands that my interests and talents lie with engineering and mechanics, you don't need to take it upon yourself to chastise me when none is needed nor appreciated."

"And that has always been the crux of it, Samuel." Grace's voice was becoming louder and the pitch of it quite piercing. "You are stubborn to the core and irresponsible as well!" When her fists hit the tabletop, Drew jumped in her chair. Grace was not only beautiful, but equally obnoxious and rude. Her aura now was completely black and swirling fast about her.

"I see I can still easily rile your sensibilities, Grace. It appears neither of us has changed much over the years."

Everyone at the table was quiet, although no one but Drew appeared the least surprised or distressed by Grace's outburst. The young woman slowly picked up her napkin, wiped her perfect mouth, and in a very calm voice stated, "Well, you may rue the day when my name is on a brass plate outside my office door, engraved with the title of Vice President of your father's bank."

"I have no doubt that day will come, and I will be the first to lift a toast to your great success. As a matter of fact, let's all lift our glasses here and now. To Grace: we all wish you great success and may the banking world never rue the day you stormed the doors, taking them all by surprise."

Everyone lifted their glasses toward the young woman, murmuring "to Grace, to Grace," with the exception of Grace, her eyes now as stormy as her aura.

The awkward toast completed, Sam took another helping of each dish, then passed them on around the table. Drew helped herself to more as well, and as she caught his eye, he smiled. She would have thought Sam's aura would be clouded from the tension, but it was shining as bright as the reflected colors on the wall. Glancing at Grace, she saw the young woman trying desperately to calm herself.

Claire had seemed oblivious to the strong emotions expressed by Grace and never addressed her during lunch. Neither Sam's mother nor Baroness Duval appeared in any way distressed by the heated banter between their children, but merely went about chatting and eating with slight smiles on their faces. It was most curious.

Drew had thought that upon meeting Grace she might feel jealous, especially upon first seeing the chic and confident woman. Drew did think Grace had some hopes of a blooming romance, combining a love of banking and a marriage to Sam, and while that might have been true on her part, it was obvious Sam had no feelings in either regard. What Drew felt now was a pang of sympathy for the young woman.

Taking a walk with Sam later in the day, Drew could not help commenting on the discussion at lunch. "I felt badly for you today. Why did Grace attack you? It certainly seemed poor manners on her part. Although, I do admit, I felt a little sorry for her as well."

"What? Grace attack me? You mean the razzing? We've been doing something similar since we were old enough to talk. Actually, before we could talk, we used to exchange barbs that included the pulling of hair and gnashing of teeth. I probably still have a few scars. I tell you, she was as fierce then as she is now."

"Your mother seemed to have found the conversation almost amusing. It must have brought back memories of those childhood disagreements. Claire, on the other hand, didn't appear particularly fond of Grace. Or is that my imagination?"

"You are, as always, a canny observer. Claire is not fond of nor has she ever been friends with Grace. Grace certainly attempted to strike up a friendship with her, but I think only as a way to stay close to the family."

"You mean close to you?"

"Perhaps. Well, probably." Sam smiled and blushed. "I think Grace and her mother always fancied a match between us. Can you imagine being married to such a person? I think she will have more success in banking than in marriage.

"Although I do feel sorry for my father, should she really join the firm. But he very clearly understands the woman. He gave me a ring before we left for London, letting me know I would probably be ambushed today before we even picked up our forks. We had a chuckle." Sam laughed. "And he was right!"

Sam put his arm around Drew's shoulder, giving her a light squeeze. "And thanks for being here. I especially enjoyed seeing you choke on your peas. Very supportive on your part."

Drew laughed, understanding that Sam's childhood acquaintance would never be anything more than a thorn in his side. She stopped short of asking herself what *she* might want to be to Sam. He had told her last Christmas that he hoped they would become more than friends, that he was looking at a cottage to buy, one not far from her grandparents. While she was sincerely fond of Sam, and sometimes felt they might eventually become more than friends, she had her immediate sights set on her future at the railway. With that in mind, she might not be so different from Grace after all.

CHAPTER 5

A DANCING DOG – TUESDAY, MARCH 18

Mara had informed Drew that Monday would be her assigned day to clean the vicarage. But Drew felt it was only kind to give the new clergyman at least another day to find his footing in his new home. He had only arrived the Friday before, so how much cleaning would really be needed?

Drew arrived at the vicarage just before seven. She could hear the music before she reached the gate, saxophones and maybe trumpets. Since opera was the preferred music they listened to at home, Drew wasn't sure what type of music was emanating from the open windows of the house.

Passing through the front gate, she admired the newly cleared gardens and propped her bike against the wooden rails. She walked up the steps and knocked twice at the door. There was no response, which wasn't surprising since the music was so loud.

She made her way back down the steps and walked over to the open window of the parlor. She was about to yell a greeting, but at the sight of a young man with burnished copper hair dancing with a large dog with fur of the same color, her words lay silent in her throat. The dog was on his hind legs, front paws in the man's hands as they moved to the music. Drew thought the smile on the dog's face was as broad as the man's. She smiled as well, waiting for a pause in the music to make her presence known.

"Hello there!" she yelled. In unison, the dog and the man looked toward the window.

"Ah, good day to you as well. And who might you be?" asked the man, dropping the dog's paws to the floor, allowing the animal to run pell-mell to the window, barking at Drew.

Drew backed up slightly and said, "I'm Drew Davies. I am hired by the church to clean the vicarage and help tend the gardens. If you are the new vicar, I thought perhaps you might have a moment to talk about a schedule that would be convenient for you and to see if the gardens are to your liking . . ."

"It's sound of you to stop by. Come round to the front door, I'll turn down the music and let you in. And stop barking, Rudy. Pay him no mind as he is a gentle soul."

Being let into the house, Drew could barely keep a look of astonishment from her face. The sitting room looked as though a tornado had come through.

Seeing her glance about the room, Liam said, "Do excuse the disaster. I haven't quite settled in as yet." He moved quickly from the sofa to the side table, picking up shirts, socks, plates and cups, and several books from the floor, then stood looking at Drew with full arms and a disarming smile.

She couldn't help smiling in return. He was not like any clergyman Drew had ever seen. "No reason to apologize. As you say, you have just moved in. And remember, I will be here once a week to tidy up and clean, which includes washing any dishes in the sink . . . or on tables or the floor. I would not be doing the laundry and would not know what to do for Rudy."

At the sound of his name, the shaggy dog moved to his master's side, looking up to his face, seemingly hoping the dancing might continue. "Do you like dogs, Miss Davies?" asked Liam.

"I have never been around dogs, although I have a big orange cat named Vesuvi."

"Well then, it is time you and Rudy were introduced properly. Rudy, please go introduce yourself to Miss Davies."

Rudy walked over to Drew, maintaining eye contact and a dog smile, sat down before her, and lifted his right paw.

"Go ahead. Shake his paw, otherwise he'll think you don't like him."

Drew didn't have to lean too far down to gently grasp the large dog's offering and said, "It's very nice to meet you, Rudy. I do hope you like your new home."

From somewhere deep in his throat, Rudy responded with a solitary "*woof*" and then walked back to stand beside the young man.

"Well, now that you have met the master of the house, let me formally introduce myself. Vicar O'Neill, or I suppose I should say, Liam O'Neill. I do hope that you, and everyone else, will call me Liam."

"And I am Miss Davies, or should I say, Drew Davies, your part-time housekeeper and gardener. And I do hope that you, like everyone else, will call me Drew."

"A pleasure to meet you, Miss Davies. Please come to the kitchen, and we can have tea and discuss a schedule."

Liam moved toward the kitchen, juggling his assortment of clothes, books, and dishes.

"Why don't you give me the dishes, and you can take care of your clothes and books. I will put the kettle on and start the tea. I am very familiar with this kitchen, unless you have rearranged it to better suit you."

"I assure you, Miss Davies—I mean, Drew—that nothing has been moved." And off he went to put his possessions where they belonged.

When he returned to the kitchen, they sat at the table as the tea steeped. "I came two or three times a week for the previous vicar, but that was because I made him his breakfast and lunch, both of which I left for him to eat at his leisure, as he was always asleep when I was here. I am happy to do the same, make you breakfast and lunch, if that is your preference."

"I would never expect you to cook for me. I think I may actually enjoy cooking for myself. And, of course, I realize that, as it seems all women's church auxiliaries are prone to do, I will not be in want of provided meals. I'm told they will appear at least twice a week. Now whether I choose to eat those meals will remain to be seen. Rudy, however, always seems to relish whatever the good ladies conjure up, and he certainly eats his fair share. That, by the way, is a secret not to be divulged to the kind ladies. I doubt they would appreciate their efforts being eaten by a dog."

"Oh, of course! Your secret is safe with me. So, no cooking is required. Do you want me to come straighten up and clean more than once a week?"

"Well, I will share another secret with you. Which is known to those who know me well, but again, the ladies of the auxiliary might find it unbecoming of their clergyman. I am known to make a *hames* of my surroundings."

"A . . . hames?" asked Drew.

"A proper mess of things. I am very clean, mind you, just not particular about where I lay and leave my belongings. Although I will try my best to be considerate, it may work well for you to come twice a week to keep the house in order."

"That is fine with me. I would need to come before I begin my job at nine o'clock. Are there two mornings a week that you might be out and about, say, around seven, or in your study where I won't disturb you?"

"I don't have a particular schedule during my week, other than devoting part of each day to my church duties and preparing my Sunday homilies. If you don't mind that I keep myself in my office here while you are about cleaning and such, you are most welcome to come at seven o'clock, twice a week. Would, say, Mondays and Thursdays work for your schedule, Miss Davies?"

"Ie, that should be fine. And I will work quietly so you will not be disturbed."

"No need to be quiet, I assure you. I work best with my music on, and as you heard, it can be loud, though I will keep it tamped down while you are cleaning. It is usually only as loud as today when Rudy and I are dancing," he said, reaching down to scratch Rudy's large head.

"Believe me, Vicar O'Neill, the music will be welcomed, as all we listen to in my cottage is opera. Also, I still need to finish up the gardens. The front beds are ready for planting but there are two areas, the sides and around the back, that still need some prepping. Would you mind if I come this Saturday morning to do that? I would not need to be inside for any reason."

"Yes, of course, and if it is alright with you, I may join you. Do you know if I am responsible for the gardens and whatever is to be done with them? I know nothing about planting and such."

"If it isn't something you are interested in doing, I am happy to keep them up, planting, weeding, and harvesting, but it will depend on what Mrs. Roberts has in mind. I will ring her and tell you what she says on Saturday. That is, if I see you."

"A good plan, Miss Davies, and do plan to see me. I would rather be out of doors than inside, and any reason or excuse for Rudy and myself to do so suits me well. My formal church duties don't begin until Easter Sunday so I have the time."

Drew wondered if his engaging smile ever left his face. Taking up her satchel, she walked over to Rudy and gave him some pets as she said her goodbyes. "See you on Saturday then. Oh, and do please call me Drew." Drew found she was smiling as she swung her satchel across her body and took up her bike. What a surprise to find such a lighthearted and friendly pastor. It certainly changed her opinion of a typical church vicar. Saturday should be interesting as well as productive. She hoped Rudy would join them, and maybe the music could be heard from the opened windows.

CHAPTER 6

GARDENING AT THE VICARAGE – SATURDAY, MARCH 22

The balmy March morning found Drew and the young vicar down on their knees in front of the garden beds. Tall mounds of overgrowth from years of disinterest and neglect had been cleared by Drew and raked into large piles which had been taken away the week before by men Mara had conscriped to do her bidding.

Drew had borrowed Granda's lorry again and this time added extra gardening gloves and another trowel to her assortment of tools. Granda's larger pair of gloves were a perfect fit for Liam. Rudy's paws were already muddy from digging in the beds, something Liam would have to put a stop to if he wanted his gardens to produce vegetables and flowers.

"I love the smell of moist earth and seeing so many worms; that is an indication that the soil is rich, and your plants should grow well. Of course, some chicken manure would be good fertilizer too. Have you given any thought to what you want to plant and where?" asked Drew.

"I might remind you, Drew, I really meant it when I said I have no knowledge of how to grow anything in dirt. However, I feel confident you might have ideas and suggestions," teased Liam.

"Of course, I do, Vicar O'Neill . . . er, Liam," said Drew with a modest smile. "As an example, in our gardens at home Nonna and I plant primarily vegetables. Even though the war is over, we are still on rations, and our victory gardens are an important source of food.

"Around the vegetables, we plant our flowers that repel insects and attract birds and bees. We have a small greenhouse, too, and plant seeds, the ones that can be gathered from last year's plants, and pot them in late February or early March."

"What type of seeds do you plant?" asked Liam, whose nose was now smudged with dirt. Drew wasn't sure if his question was born of sincere interest or he was teasing her again.

"We start corn, squash, pumpkins, tomatoes, cucumbers, beets, beans, and peas. A number of potatoes and onions are kept over each year. After the potatoes grow eyes, we divide them and after the onions sprout, we plant them directly into the ground in late April.

"And we gather the seeds from the fading flowers in the fall, such as nasturtiums, sweet peas, and zinnias. Flowers like poppies reseed themselves and come back year after year. And of course, bulbs, like tulips and such, do the same."

"Is your garden as large as you make it sound, to grow all of that?"

"In the last several years, because of the shortages, Granda and Nonna have made our gardens a little larger every year. And not everything grows equally well every season. What I never really understand, beyond the fact of needing water—but not too much and more on sunny and hot days—is that some years the tomatoes and corn just don't do very well. Other years we have a prolific crop, and come fall, we furiously can it all for the winter. And we have chickens as well, so that is a help." Drew's nose was itchy, and she assumed was as grubby as Liam's.

"Sounds like a lot of work. And you say you like it, this digging around in the dirt as we are doing today?"

"There is almost nothing I would rather do. Gardening is like a meditation, one with great benefits. When I am in the gardens, my mind doesn't think about anything else, and because I am outside and it is hard work, it feels all that much better. And then, to see it all bloom and grow from just a tiny seed or sprout, a bulb or cutting, is exciting. It's a miracle really. And then we get to enjoy the flowers and eat the vegetables. What could be more wonderful? Surely a clergyman like yourself can see the miracle of it all."

"Well, I can't really imagine that these long empty gardens will be full and colorful in the months ahead. But, Miss Davies, with your expert tending I trust they will. Did you talk with Mrs. Roberts about helping?"

"Ie, I forgot to tell you. I spoke with her last evening, and she said since you don't want me to prepare any meals, if you would like my assistance with the gardens, that would be a suitable exchange, and my rate of pay will stay the same. And she suggested that perhaps you might want to learn the ins and outs of weeding and watering so you can take some responsibility for them too. She doesn't think I will have the time needed to keep them all in order, but really, I don't think she wants to pay me for all the time." It was Drew's turn to smile again.

Looking up at the young man beside her, she watched him reach up and scratch his copper curls, saying, "Hmmm, . . . She said that, did she? I thought I was called here to shepherd my flock, not feed it."

"Don't worry, Liam. I am very used to gardening quickly, and I won't let yours suffer. These beds were such a sad eyesore, and after all the clearing work I've done, and all the planting ahead, I want to see them prosper and grow. I'll show you the difference between the weeds to be pulled and what stays in the ground. You really need to stay ahead of the weeds, you know."

"I *don't* know, but I'll give it my best effort and will pull up the nasty things when I take Rudy outside. That sounds like a good arrangement."

Drew stood up to gather the debris into piles when she saw Rudy digging into the bed beside Liam. "And speaking of Rudy, you can't allow him to dig in the gardens like that. We may have to put up a short fence. That is, unless you can assure me you can keep him out of all the beds once they're planted."

"I doubt I could keep him from digging. So, I suppose a fence might be the thing. Can we talk about that later? I am more than hungry, and it certainly must be time for lunch. The generous ladies have already graced me with an overabundance of food."

Drew moved next to Liam and held out her hand. He looked at the brown wiggling worm in her palm and lifted it onto his own hand before laying it back on top of the soil, saying, "We can make a sketch while we eat and decide where to plant everything."

Drew liked that about the young man: that he was hungry, seemed perpetually good natured, and he suggested making a sketch. Leaving their gardening tools where they lay, they removed their gloves and walked into the kitchen. They washed their hands and splashed water onto their dirty faces, and each other, laughing all the while.

Drew set the kettle on and Liam took, what looked to Drew, all the food the larder contained and placed it on the table. As they gathered the plates, cups, and cutlery, Drew realized she hoped she had made a friend and hoped he thought so as well.

They sat at the table enjoying the full plates before them. "If this is the type of food the ladies are bringing you, you certainly won't starve. It's quite good," she said between bites. "Mind if I have another spoonful?"

"I do agree. Another helping all around." Liam took the serving spoon and dipped into the glass casserole dish full of something creamy with potatoes, scooped up a large amount, and dropped it squarely onto Drew's plate. He then secured another helping, bent down, and placed it on Rudy's plate on the floor. Lastly, he helped himself to an amount equally as large while Drew refilled their teacups.

"Perhaps they are giving me their very best meals from their ration supplies to make a good first impression, and in due course they will only bring dried potatoes and their family leftovers," said Liam, his mouth once again full.

"No worries there. These women pride themselves on providing their holy men with the best that comes from ration recipes. I know, because I saw what appeared in Vicar Hughes's larder on a weekly basis. He ate so little that I tossed out most of the food or ate some myself before it went bad. I think the Women's Auxiliary will be very pleased they finally have a vicar who appreciates their efforts."

"You are eating rather vigorously yourself, Miss Davies. You and Rudy are my equals in that regard, would you not agree?"

Drew choked on her food and wondered if she was being unladylike. But the thought drifted quickly from her mind, and she just smiled and saluted Liam with her teacup raised before taking a sip.

Appetites satiated, they leaned back into their chairs. Drew asked, "Why did you decide to accept a post in Wales rather than Ireland?"

Liam turned and looked out the window for some time before saying, "I had several interim placements before I was called here, three different parishes for several months at a time as part of my training, and my last placement was for a year, all in Ireland. Two of those congregations requested I remain with them, but . . . I felt I needed a change. I love Ireland. It will always be my home. And like most places people call home, it holds sad as well as fond memories. But it was time to leave, leave the past behind and begin my life apart from where I grew up." Running a hand through his hair, he looked at Drew, saying, "Does that make sense?"

"Ie, of course it does. Sometimes people choose to make a new beginning for themselves, and other times people are forced to make one. Certainly after the war many people whose families were fractured and displaced have started over, and that does not always mean going back home. Did the war figure into your decision?" Drew asked quietly.

"No, not in a direct way. My parents died when I was ten years old. I was then sent to live with my da's older sister, Theda, and her friend, Eireann. They are wonderful women and gave me everything I should have needed to grow up healthy and happy. But sometimes the pain of missing my parents was overwhelming. I think that is the reason I went into the church. I was looking for answers, for reasons why God would take them from me. Even though I wasn't alone, but rather loved and cared for, I also felt I was missing pieces of my life.

"As I grew older, I became angry and resentful. I got into trouble at school. I was a bully, and every time I got into fisticuffs, I always hoped the other boy would knock me out cold, hurt me badly, maybe even kill me. I gave my aunts a rough go of it. The vicar in our parish stepped up alongside me and became someone I could talk with. He would take me fishing on quiet lakes, spending hours on the water, mostly in silence, until my anger abated and I would feel safe enough to let my guard down.

"At first, he just talked, mostly about fishing, but then about how he understood why I was angry and hurt. Initially, I had felt trapped in that small boat. I could not walk on water, so I just had to sit there and listen. He prayed with me one day, and I broke down sobbing. He just kept on praying, and after his amen, we just went on fishing. I learned I could be honest with him, be myself and pour out all my feelings, including my resentment toward God. Over time, the diligent compassion of this man allowed me to share the feelings of confusion and anger I constantly carried with me and the excruciating pain from the loss of my family. He became my counselor and friend. By the time school ended, I had found peace enough to regain my bearings. That kind man saved my life.

"For many years, even throughout university, he continued to mentor me, and when I told him I thought I wanted to enter the church and become a clergyman, I don't think he was surprised. Nor was he convinced that I was making that choice because I truly felt a calling. And honestly, to this day, I am not sure it *is* my calling, but it *is* where I feel I can help those that are lost and hurting much the same as I was. If that is a calling, then I am in the right place. And if it isn't, time will help me sort it out. I hope here in Mumbles I can make a difference, find a new home and a community with people I come to care about and want to serve, and who care for me in return." Liam closed his eyes then and sat very still. When he opened them and looked at Drew, he saw tears in her eyes.

"I'm so sorry, Drew, I hope I have not upset you with my long tale. I seldom share any of that and certainly not with someone I hardly know. But I thank you for listening. I think that you are truly my first friend here, and I cannot think of a better one."

Drew dabbed her eyes and smiled at him. "I'm not upset, Liam. My tears are because your story resonates in so many ways with my own. I, too, lost my parents, including my older brother. I was just a young child, but the pain of that loss is with me every day. My father's parents raised me, and I love them more dearly because of it. They are my family, my only family, and I have a good life. But you and I, and those like us, will always feel the pain of loss and deep sorrow.

"I hope, too, that you find a home here, Liam, a family within your congregation and among friends you meet here in Mumbles. I am very honored that I am your first friend here. I think we will be fast friends who share a bond, an understanding that allows us to care for others a little more than most because we connect with them more deeply. Perhaps that is both our callings."

"Thank you, Drew. And I acknowledge the privilege of you sharing your sorrow as well. Here's to friendship." Together they wiped their eyes, smiled beyond the tears, and held their cups up to one another, saluting new friends and new beginnings.

The kitchen set to rights, Drew and Liam returned to the garden and finished clearing the remainder of the beds. Late afternoon was setting in when he helped Drew gather up all the garden implements and stow them into the bed of the lorry.

"Might I come in and wash my hands and face before I leave, Liam?"

"Well, of course. I'd say we had quite a productive day, though we never sketched out the plan for the garden. What if you made the plan according to what you think is best, as I'm sure it will be excellent? Then when does the planting begin?"

"I will let you know. And if anything shows up in the garden, don't pull it out until you show me."

"I'm not sure I could tell a weed from a rose, but I'll keep watch."

Having cleaned herself up, Drew walked to the door to take her leave when Rudy trotted in front of her, sat firmly in place at the door, and began whining.

"Look! Rudy wants to go out and do more gardening!"

"Actually, he doesn't want you to leave. He has enjoyed making a new friend as much as I have."

Liam gave a low bow, saying, "Rudy and I both thank you, Miss Davies, for your friendship and assistance in learning about dirt."

"You are both very welcome, and I'll see you next week. Perhaps I'll even have some seeds to plant. That will be your next gardening lesson, Vicar O'Neill."

PASTA FRIDAY ON SATURDAY – MARCH 22

I n no hurry to arrive home, Drew drove slowly as she made her way from the vicarage. The late afternoon breeze helped cool her thoughts as she puzzled over the swirl of emotions that filled her mind.

Approaching the cottage, she knew Nonna and Serena were there, beginning the dough for the pasta, cooking something delicious to crown it, and listening to Italian arias on the phonograph. Drew stopped some distance from the cottage, stepped off her bike, and walked the remainder of the way. When she arrived, she leaned her bicycle against the wall of the shed and then leaned her back against it as well. She stood looking at the cottage gardens and thinking of all she and Liam had accomplished.

Breathing deeply, she tried to calm her stomach, as it seemed to turn round and round with her thoughts. She finally pushed herself away from the wall and made her way to the kitchen door.

"*Buonasera*, Drew Girl," greeted Serena, her nonna's oldest and dearest friend and Drew's godmother. "The pasta needs your strong hands."

Giving them both smiles and silent hugs, Drew washed her hands, donned her apron, and began rolling the dough. She said nothing to the women as her hands found traction, pushing the dough in all directions across Nonna's treasured pasta board. Drew felt her feelings flow through her fingers into the dough, hoping it would taste of new friendship and kindness.

Nonna and Serena exchanged looks at Drew's silence but continued humming along with the music as they rolled balls of meat, the aroma of oregano and garlic filling the air.

"Tonight, we are making *polpette con salsa di panna,* meatballs in cream sauce, so please cut the pasta into linguine," instructed Nonna.

"It smells as though yesterday was a good day in the ration lines," Drew said, cutting the thinly rolled sheet into strips.

"It was, and that is why we changed pasta Friday to today. I was also able to exchange some fabric for two small parcels of meat. The farmer's daughter is getting married and needed material for a dress, so we bartered, and everyone went away happy." Serena smiled. "Although I cannot attest to exactly what type of meat we are going to be eating, it is making succulent meatballs."

She was a dressmaker and over the years had accumulated a large trunk and several chests of drawers full of all types of beautiful fabrics. Due to the ongoing reality of food shortages and rationing, she often exchanged her skills and her fabric for food or goods. Drew had often been the fortunate recipient of beautiful garments designed and made specifically for her by her benevolent godmother.

"And Granda and Henri . . . remember Henri? The Frenchman who sold Granda the beautiful wine goblets? They foraged for mushrooms this morning, and yesterday I used my rations for butter and flour. We are going to have a delicious meal tonight," added Nonna.

Drew smiled as she hung the long strands of linguine onto the rungs of the wood drying rack. Once again, she took up the long *mattanello* and rolled out another sheet of paper-thin pasta. Working alongside these dear women was always a place of pleasure and solace. Their presence was especially welcome this evening.

"How are the gardens at the vicarage coming along? Those overgrown beds are a lot of work for just one person," said Nonna.

"Vicar O'Neill worked alongside me the entire day, and time went by quickly. The front and side beds are cleared and almost ready to be planted."

"Well, that was kind of him. And how did you find the man? Was he a help or a hindrance," asked Serena as she gently placed the meatballs into the sauce.

Drew felt her stomach tilt again in remembrance. "He was quite handy once I showed him what needed to be done. He pulled out the heavier overgrowth and carried stacks of brush to the piles as I cleared and raked the soil. And there was an abundance of worms. Liam was thrilled to see them, as he enjoys fishing.

"And he has a dog. A big red fellow named Rudy. They listen to loud jazz music and actually dance together! They make quite a happy pair."

"So, we know the new vicar is willing to help garden, has a dog, and likes to dance and fish. And what does this dancing vicar look like, Drew Girl? Is he as young as we hear?" asked Serena.

"I would guess him to be nearing thirty. He stands half a head above me. I think he enjoys life . . . but I sense a sadness about him as well. His blue eyes are kind and full of mirth and his dark red hair is thick and wavy; it seems to glow."

"Ah, like the flame on the head of an apostle. That is certainly a fitting picture," said Serena. "And did you have much conversation as you worked the gardens?"

"We talked away the day, as we seem to have much in common. He also lost his parents in an accident when he was a boy and was raised by his aunts Theda and Eireann. There is a trace of melancholy in his spirit, I can see it in his aura. But he is quick to laugh and tease, and we agreed that today we became friends. It was really such a glorious day, and that is why I don't understand my stomach being all twisted and my thoughts keep returning to his smile."

Drew turned with a crooked smile toward the women to find them standing stock still and staring at her, cooking utensils in hand, with raised eyebrows and smiles of their own.

"That is sometimes the way of things, Drew," said Nonna, stepping forward to place a hand on her arm. "A wry smile and bright blue eyes can turn a girl's heart in a moment's time."

"Well, it's not my heart that is turning, but my stomach. I'm not sure I'll be able to eat dinner . . . and it smells so wonderful."

Serena joined Nonna at Drew's side. "Well, we cannot, even due to the addition of a handsome friend into your life, have you miss eating these prized meatballs. You sit down at the table, and we'll make you a nice cup of tea to calm your stomach. And breathe, Drew, it will calm you as well. We will cut the remainder of the pasta." Nonna nodded in agreement as she set the kettle on.

Drew did as she was told and closed her eyes as she breathed deeply. Vesuvi jumped onto her lap, and soon she had downed two cups of tea and did indeed feel better.

"Ah, your aura is settling now," said Nonna.

"Ie, I do feel calmer. Thank you both. I think I might just go lie on my bed till dinner. I am definitely not going to miss out on these meatballs."

Drew left the table and walked into her small bedroom, Vesuvi following close behind. She heard Serena and Nonna's quiet chatter as she lay down on her bed and closed her eyes, her cat cuddled into her. And what she saw was Liam in the gardens, his broad smile and laughing eyes looking back at her. Although her stomach had settled, she felt confused and restless and wondered how she could have such feelings for a man she had just met. Why had she been so comfortable sharing so much of herself with this stranger?

She also found herself puzzled as to why she had never felt such a surge of emotion when she was with Sam. Maybe it was because she and Sam had known each other for so many years now. What did any of it mean?

Next thing she knew, Nonna was beside her, gently rousing her from sleep and telling her it was time to eat. She found her mouth watering, smelling the food she knew was on the table. Eating always helped her feel stronger and ready for anything, hopefully even being a good friend.

CHAPTER 8

A FATEFUL JOURNEY – SUNDAY, MARCH 23

It had been a day and forever ago that she and Eireann had been on a train together. Theda knew Eireann still occasionally traveled by herself up and down Ireland, doing what she did, but it had been years since Theda heard the hypnotic clack-clacking of the wheels on the tracks. It always sounded like adventure to her.

She glanced over at her companion of so many years, soundly sleeping, and felt a thrill knowing they were together on this journey to see their nephew Liam in his new posting. She could not quite say "new home," because it was probably much too early for him to know if that is what Wales would become. And if he did stay, she would miss him being so far away from them.

Eireann stirred beside her. "How much longer before we arrive in Swansea? I'm stiff as a board sitting for so long."

"According to the schedule, we should be there within the next twenty minutes," replied Theda, patting Eireann's restless hands.

"Ah, and look up front. Just what we needed to speed the time: a cup of tea coming our way."

A stout man in the railway uniform of a restaurant car attendant was walking down the aisle offering passengers tea. Eireann and Theda sat up a little straighter, ready to accept the welcome treat.

"Ladies?" the man asked, nodding toward the tray of small porcelain cups.

"Yes, please. We'll both kindly accept a cup of your thoughtful offering," said Theda.

The attendant nodded again, handing a cup first to Eireann, who sat next to the window, and then to Theda. He nodded once more and moved on to the remainder of the passengers in their sparsely occupied carriage.

"This English tea is quite bitter but wet at least. I really expected the service to be a notch higher on the Great Western Line," commented Eireann, drinking hers down.

Theda finished hers as well, then stood and set the empty cup upright in the corner of her seat. "I'm going to use the facilities before we arrive. I'll hurry back, as we should be pulling into the station shortly."

Theda exited her seat and reached the back of the carriage just as Eireann realized something was terribly amiss. She began experiencing muscle spasms and an uncontrollable arching in her neck and back. Her breathing was becoming difficult, and pain was setting in throughout her body. Fear set in as well, and her heart began to race, the beating irregular and intense. *Why hadn't Theda returned yet?*

As her body spasmed and the pain intensified, she had the startling realization that she had been poisoned. She had ingested poison in the nefarious offering of tea and would most likely succumb to suffocation before they arrived in Swansea. *Oh, where was Theda?*

Eireann remembered she was sitting on her coat. The deep pocket on the left side was accessible to her, and with trembling hands, she found the large handkerchief she always kept there. Hands jerking now, she struggled to wrap the almost-empty teacup into the cloth and plunged it deep inside the large pocket of her coat. At least this remnant of the circumstances of her death would hopefully be found. Her eyes were full of tears as she realized what a terrible inconvenience this would cause Theda and would completely spoil Liam's first service on Easter. She had thought they had given up looking for her years ago.

She lay back against the cushioned seat and was gone, her pocket containing the only message she had time to leave.

Theda spent a great deal more time at the sink and mirror than she intended but felt her reflection was as generous as could be expected. Her heart was racing with excitement as she exited the facilities and returned to her seat next to Eireann.

"Wake up, dear one. The train is slowing, and we'll be pulling into the station shortly. I am so excited I can hardly contain myself. Eireann, wake up."

Gentle shaking was not helping to rouse her. Shaking her again and then again, Theda realized something was wrong. She began shouting at Eireann as panic took over and then heard herself crying out for help. An older gentleman from the front of the carriage quickly left his seat and approached the two women.

"Oh dear God," Theda said quietly to no one but herself. "I think she is dead."

The gentleman placed his index and second fingers to Eireann's wrist and then slowly dropped his arm saying, "Let us hope your friend has just lost consciousness. I will call the conductor immediately. We are pulling into the station and help will be found."

Theda merely nodded as she placed her arms around her dear one's shoulders and cradled her. She wanted to stop time, wanted Eireann to wake up, for them to return immediately to Ireland and not face what lay ahead. But she knew Eireann was gone, knew it in her heart. And poor Liam. He would be waiting for them, and she was so sorry for what he would find, one dead aunt and one with a broken heart.

Liam was indeed waiting on the platform to take charge of his aunts and accompany them to the vicarage. How eager he was to see these two precious women and show them his new home. He spied Drew a short distance down the platform, and they waved to one another. Liam thought she looked quite fetching in her railway uniform.

As the train came to a halt, Jonesy, the conductor, jumped from the doorway and ran inside the depot. Drew realized something was wrong and followed him as he raced into Granda's office, shouting, "There's been an incident on the train! A woman! Ring the constable!"

The conductor quickly relayed what information he could to Granda, who immediately picked up the telephone, saying to Drew and Jonesy, "Move all the passengers into the depot. No one is to leave until the police arrive and take control of the situation."

Drew, Jonesy, and Abigail, the depot's charwoman and sometime baggage attendant, rushed back to the train. Drew instructed them to go through two cars each and direct the passengers inside to wait until further notice, and to be sure no one left the depot. She would see to the afflicted woman's car.

"Drew, what is going on? Has something happened on the train?" Liam stood on the platform, his hat in his hands, looking for all the world like a lost soul.

"I'm not sure yet. But go back inside the depot. Your aunts will be escorted into the waiting area shortly. Go in, now."

"Miss! Miss! This is the carriage where the unconscious woman is. Can you come assist?" called an older gentleman.

Drew quickly climbed aboard and made her way into the carriage, the man leading her to two women, one in tears and clearly beside herself and the other still and looking quite at peace.

Kneeling in the aisle, Drew reached out and touched the crying woman's arms. "Hello, my name is Drew Davies. I am an employee of the railway, and I am here to assist you in any way I can. We have rung the authorities, and they should be here shortly. Can you tell me what happened?"

"I went to use the facilities and when I returned, I found her like this. This gentleman took her pulse and said perhaps she had just fainted, but I know she is gone. I have no idea what happened, only that she was fine when I left her."

"How long were you gone, Mrs. . . . .?

"Maybe ten minutes, perhaps a bit longer. I am Theda O'Neill, and this is my companion, Eireann Swan."

Drew felt her own heart stop at hearing the names. These were Liam's beloved aunts, come to celebrate with him. She felt hot tears rise in her eyes. Tamping down her emotions, she said, "Miss O'Neill, I am acquainted with your nephew, Liam. He is waiting inside the depot lobby for you. Do you want me to take you to him or bring him to you?"

"I just want everyone to go away and let me be with my Eireann. How can I face Liam and bring him such grief at a time that should be so joyous for him? I do not know what to do."

Drew could hear commotion behind her and knew the police had most likely arrived. She also knew that after determining if Liam's aunt was dead, the body would be taken away.

"Drew, Chief Inspector Lewis has arrived," said Howard, making his way up the aisle. "He's right behind me. His men are dealing with the passengers. What have you found here?"

Drew stepped away from Miss O'Neill before answering. "The woman appears to have died. Her name is Eireann Swan, and the other woman is Theda O'Neill. These women are Vicar Liam's aunts, Granda! Come to stay at the vicarage with him till after Easter. I told Liam to go inside and wait. He must be extremely worried not seeing his aunts among the other passengers. I know the police will eventually speak with him, but I need to go tell him what has happened before they do."

Before Drew could take her leave to go find Liam, he appeared behind her and slipped quickly past Granda and the Chief Inspector to his aunts' sides.

"Oh, dear Liam," said Theda in a thin, faraway voice. "I am so very sorry. I did not know Eireann was ill. Whatever could have happened in just the short time I was away from her?"

Liam took his aunt into his arms, patting her back as he looked askance over her shoulder at Drew. Chief Inspector Lewis held off, giving Liam and Theda some little time to compose themselves. Drew knew death brought such a sense of helplessness in the midst of great loss: pain, confusion, fear, and even physical responses. Guilt and anger are never far behind.

"Miss O'Neill, I am Chief Inspector Lewis. A physician is to arrive shortly to examine Miss Swan, and he will confirm if she has indeed passed."

Drew did not know if Miss O'Neill heard anything that Chief Inspector Lewis had related. But she did see Liam, still holding his aunt, nod.

"Auntie Theda, sit down across from Eireann, and we'll wait for the doctor. I will not leave your side, and I know these good people will assist us in any way they can." Liam sat Theda onto the seat across the aisle from Eireann as he remained standing.

As if on cue, a stern-looking man carrying a black leather physician's bag entered the train car. "Excuse me, excuse me," he said, pushing past the people standing in the aisle as he made his way to where Eireann's body lay askew on the seat.

"Hello, Chief. What have we got here?" asked the doctor, placing his bag beside the body and removing a stethoscope. Not giving an introduction nor waiting for a response from the chief inspector, the physician examined Eireann's body and declared, "This woman has died and probably within the last hour." He glanced from face to face. "Can anyone tell me what happened?"

"My name is Liam O'Neill, Vicar O'Neill, and this is my aunt, Eireann Swan. She and my other aunt, Miss Theda O'Neill, just arrived on the train. My aunt Theda says she returned to their seats from the lavatory and was then unable to rouse Miss Swan."

"Hmm . . . Miss O'Neill, was your sister ill or in any distress that you know of during the trip or before you boarded the train?"

Ignoring the fact that the doctor presumed the two women to be sisters, Theda replied, "No. She was well, and we were both very excited about the train trip. We were enjoying the scenery and looking forward to being met by our nephew, Liam. Eireann was fine, just fine." Theda covered her face with her hands and began sobbing.

Liam dropped to his knees and put his arms about her shoulders. "And what happens now? Where will she be taken?"

"She'll be transported to hospital, where she'll be attended to by the medical examiner. If her death is deemed to have occurred by natural causes, and I would surmise at this point she most likely suffered a severe heart attack or stroke, you may have her body removed for funeral care. All that will take at least until tomorrow, as the medical examiner must complete his report before the certificate of death can be signed. The hospital will ring you when her body is ready to be moved, probably late morning or early afternoon.

Liam stood and turned to the doctor. "Please have them ring the vicarage in Mumbles. My aunt will be there with me."

Theda continued crying, her words muffled and difficult to understand, but Drew thought she heard her say, "I cannot believe this happened, not now, not after so long a time." No one else seemed to pay her words any mind other than Liam, who kept trying to reassure her that it would be alright, that he was taking her back to the vicarage and there was nothing they could do until tomorrow.

Before the doctor left the train, Chief Inspector Lewis instructed the physician to notify him immediately when the cause of death was determined. Then Lewis turned to Miss O'Neill. "You said when you returned from the lavatory, you found Miss Swan unconscious and you were not able to wake her, but that she was fine minutes before. Did she say anything to you during the trip to indicate she wasn't feeling well?"

Theda collected herself before replying. "As I just told the doctor, she seemed fine. As a matter of fact, we both had just had a cup of tea. Eireann drank hers quickly, and I finished mine before going to the facilities, as we knew we would be arriving at the station soon. Absolutely nothing seemed amiss."

Through the window, Liam, Drew, and Theda watched two men from the ambulance service arrive and board the train. They unfolded their stretcher on the floor of the aisle and carefully lifted Eireann onto the heavy canvas cloth as Theda sat clutching Liam's hand, crying quietly.

"We are very sorry for your loss, Miss O'Neill," began the chief inspector, "and while this is a difficult time, I'll need to speak with you again tomorrow to take a lengthier statement. By then, you may remember something you can't recall right now, as you are greatly shocked. The other passengers are inside the station, and my officers and I will question them all, but you may leave with your nephew. I understand that we can find you at the vicarage," said Lewis as he closed his notebook and nodded to Liam. With that, Chief Inspector Lewis and another officer left the train and headed into the station to speak to the other passengers.

Drew saw that the officer had handed Lewis two china teacups and was carrying three more in his own hands. Obviously, everyone in the carriage had been served tea.

Drew, Liam, and Theda stepped off the carriage and stood on the platform. Watching as the doors to the ambulance closed, Theda grabbed Liam's arm and pleaded, "Oh Liam, I can't let her go alone. I need to go with her."

"She isn't there, Auntie, she is here with you, as always. Let me find your bags, and we'll make our way to the vicarage." Liam turned to Drew. "And thank you, Drew, for staying with us."

"Of course, of course. I am so very sorry for you both. I'll come by tomorrow to see what you might need. Good evening, Miss O'Neill. Please let me know if there is anything I can do."

Drew watched as they walked to the line of luggage the porter had placed along the platform. Theda pointed to three bags, and Liam placed the smallest under his arm, then picked up the other two. His aunt grasped his arm and they departed through the depot and on to the vicarage.

Drew returned immediately to the passenger car. She stood for some time at the entrance, looking all around the interior— top to bottom, side to side—and slowly walked forward, taking in all she saw, as Granda had taught her. *Be still and observe everything you see.* At the end of the car, she turned and slowly made her way back to the seats occupied by the two aunts. A mustard-colored wool coat lay across the seat Eireann had occupied. The officer must have assumed the coat belonged to Miss O'Neill and left it for her to take. But, in her distress, Theda had also left it behind. Did the coat belong to Eireann or to Theda?

Drew lifted the coat, which still seemed warm. She could feel an energy about it and realized something was in a pocket. She reached her hand into the right one and then the left. In the left pocket, she could feel fabric and something solid and oddly shaped. She sat down on the seat and examined it. The cloth was a large white linen handkerchief, embroidered with the initials *ES* in beautiful blue script. Drew carefully unwrapped the cloth, revealing a porcelain teacup. The corners of the handkerchief had been stuffed inside the cup and the edges were damp with the remains of a liquid. This was curious, thought Drew. Why would the cup be in the pocket of the coat? She meticulously rewrapped the cup and placed it into the pocket of her uniform.

Drew decided to begin from the front of the carriage again and, on her hands and knees, crawled the entire length, looking carefully round the floor and under each seat. Toward the front of the coach, she spied another teacup under a left-aisle seat next to the window. She secured this second cup, handling it carefully from the bottom edge, and placed it into her other pocket. Before she left the carriage, Drew checked the toilet and found it empty.

If all the teacups were accounted for, including the one in the pocket of the yellow coat, seven passengers had ridden in this carriage, or at least seven of them had accepted a cup of tea. Looking round one more time, she could find nothing else that could be considered evidence or out of place.

Returning to Eireann's seat, she gathered up the yellow coat, took a last look around, and exited the train. An odd feeling of disquiet followed close behind her.

CHAPTER 9

COFFEE WITH GRANDA – MONDAY, MARCH 24

It was early morning and, as Drew hoped, Granda had waited for her to have coffee with him before leaving for the station. He sat in his usual place at the head of the large wood table in the middle of the kitchen. The morning was chilly but not cold enough to burn the rationed coal or their store of wood to heat the cottage. Drew sat down, still wrapped comfortably in her worn robe with her back to the empty hearth and Granda to her left.

He took up her cup and poured her coffee as she reached for the small pitcher to add a little milk. Howard, like his granddaughter, always drank coffee in the mornings and tea for the remainder of the day. They were each thankful coffee was not rationed, as the stuff made of chicory was barely tolerable. Though good coffee was often hard to come by, Granda always found enough for their breakfast.

Several minutes passed as they sipped and thought about yesterday's tragedy. Drew knew Granda would speak when he settled what he wanted to say, and she was content to sit quietly, hands around the warm cup and Vesuvi on her lap.

"While you were back on the train, the officers questioned all the passengers one by one from the lineup on the benches. Most were locals, and after a series of questions, Lewis let them go home. He knew where they lived should he want to speak with them again.

"There were also the usual businessmen, all of them familiar to me, as they travel frequently back and forth from London or Cardiff. And then there were a few others, all from Ireland, that the Inspector directed to find lodging nearby and remain available for further questioning. I have their names." Granda pushed a piece of paper toward Drew, where she saw the names of one family of four and one other man.

"They all traveled here from Belfast and gave various reasons for landing in South Wales. I assume you might want to copy the list."

"Ie, thank you, Granda." Drew would make a copy and seek out information on the people as soon as she could.

"Anabelle found men's clothing in a lavatory, stuffed behind a toilet, and a scuffed pair of men's shoes and a railway hat in the trash bin. I passed the lot on to Lewis. The clothing was odd—it was heavily padded. Someone did not want to be recognized."

"Can we be sure the clothes were not there before the train arrived but hidden there after?" Drew asked, sliding her empty cup toward Granda.

He filled it, saying, "Annabelle doesn't remember seeing anything of the sort when she cleaned the night before, but as we know, she is sometimes scattered, so we can't be certain. But I should think she would have remembered had an unusual bundle of clothes been there last evening. I am surmising it was all done quickly by someone in disguise exiting the train as it was arriving at the station, then going into the toilet, changing quickly, hiding the clothes, and returning to the lobby where they were questioned."

"That would seem to be the most likely scenario. Hopefully someone saw the person exit the train as they headed into the depot."

They sat quietly for some moments before Granda spoke again. "Once people realized something had happened, and they were all to be detained in the lobby, it became chaotic. Someone could easily have gone to the lavatory, changed, and been back in the lobby before anyone noticed. Everyone will be questioned further and hopefully someone saw something . . . or someone."

"I'm hungry. You must be too. Let's have breakfast and then I want to show you what I found. It's in my room."

"I'll make us food, Drew Girl. You go ahead. Breakfast will be quick, then we need to head to the depot. Everyone will be worried and on edge. And I expect a Great Western inspector from London to be showing up sometime during the day. I will have Lewis with me when the questions are asked."

"I would like to be there as well," Drew said, rounding the corner to her room. She reappeared with her leather satchel and the mustard-colored coat. Drew removed the linen-wrapped cup and laid it gently on the table. She then took the other teacup from the satchel and set it some distance from the wrapped one. The coat she laid across the back of the chair next to her.

Granda put toast and preserves onto the table, eyeing what Drew had placed there. He sat down and waited for her to enlighten him.

"In all the chaos, as you say, and as the constables were questioning everyone in the lobby, I went back to the woman's carriage. This coat was still lying on the seat. To me, it still felt warm, and I could feel an energy to it. At that moment, I believed the coat belonged to Eireann Swan. I took a minute to send her light and then I gently patted down the coat and searched the two pockets, one on either side. In one of them, I found this." She gently unwrapped the teacup, being sure not to touch or smudge it.

"It was wrapped exactly as you see it, and the linen was slightly damp with what looked like tea, and it smelled slightly bitter. You can see the corners are stained from the liquid, and if you put your nose to the cup, it retains an odor as well."

Howard got up and moved around the table to where the teacup lay on its side. He stood very still, then bent down and looked at it from every angle. "Ie, I smell the bitterness. I also see the brand mark on the bottom of the cup but can't make it out."

"It says 'Ireland' just below the mark." Drew pointed to the other cup where the brand mark was clearer but an image of something was still illegible. "I put the wrapped cup in my uniform pocket and then searched the train car thoroughly, including on my hands and knees. One of Lewis's constables also found teacups. I saw him pick them up from the carriage seats and, as best as I could tell, he and Lewis left the car with five.

"I found this identical cup while I was searching the floor. It was under a left-side seat at the very front of the carriage. After checking the toilet and having another look about the carriage, I gathered up the yellow coat and both cups and left the train. In our office, I wrapped the cups, put them into a clean paper bag, and tucked them in my satchel. I laid the coat across my chair and then went to the lobby to help as I could."

"Good work, Drew Girl. We will have to turn all of this in to Chief Inspector Lewis, but only to him. Both cups need to be checked for fingerprints, and the dried liquid on the linen and the cup need to be examined."

"I know I probably read too many mystery novels, but am I wrong in thinking Eireann may have been poisoned and she left us the evidence?"

"No, Drew Girl, you are not wrong. Let's get to the station and get the lay of things before going to see Lewis. Ride in the lorry with me and bring what you have with you. You can stow your bicycle in the back."

Drew dressed hurriedly and waited for Granda at the front door. She threw the coat over her arm, carefully took up her satchel, containing possible evidence, and they quickly made their way to the station. As they drove in silence the twenty minutes north along the scenic coastline between Mumbles and Swansea, Drew could not help but wonder if another murder, somehow more personal, had found her again. With this thought, her heart ached for Liam and his aunt Theda.

DELIVERING THE EVIDENCE – MONDAY, MARCH 24

It was noon before Granda and Drew were able to leave the station and drive to the constabulary, the cups and linen handkerchief tucked safely in Drew's satchel. Granda stopped the lorry in front of the office. It took her back to last year, when they had talked with the police during the investigation into Victor Hughes's murder.

"Please leave the coat in the lorry, Granda," said Drew. She jumped out and proceeded inside while he parked.

Drew was hoping the front desk would not be manned today by Constable Swain, but as she feared, there he sat, twiddling his pencil and doodling. Did the man ever do any actual work?

"Ah, Miss Davies. And what would you be doing here today?" he said, a leering smile stretched across his face.

"The usual. Wanting to speak with your superior, Chief Inspector Lewis. Would you please tell him I am here regarding the investigation into the death of Eireann Swan?"

"And how many times do I need tell you, Miss Davies, you can talk to me the same as you could with the chief. I am an officer of the law as well, and don't you know it."

"What *I* know, Private Swain, is that you are to do as requested and let your superior know we are here." Granda always caught Swain in the middle of a less-than-appropriate comment.

Flustered, Swain leaped from his chair at the sight of Sergeant Howard Davies. "Ie, Sergeant Davies. I'll let him know. Right away, Sir."

Drew had witnessed Swain's fear of Granda a time or two before, and it always brought a smile. Her grandfather had been an officer in the railway battalion in both wars, and many men that served under him were still living in the area. These men, with the exception of a few, such as Swain, formed a brotherhood of support within the community.

Chief Inspector Lewis soon made his entrance with a salute to Granda, who saluted him in return, then the two men exchanged handshakes.

"Seeing as I saw you both yesterday, can I assume you have information about Miss Swan's death on the train?"

Drew reached into her satchel and carefully removed the paper bag, laying it gently on the counter as she explained, "There are two teacups in this bag, one wrapped in a linen handkerchief, that may be evidence of foul play in the death of Miss Swan.

"Once all the passengers and you and your officers had exited the train, I went back to the carriage to be sure there was nothing left in the car. I found a coat still lying on the seat, and in the pocket was this teacup," said Drew, carefully removing the one wrapped in linen. "The bottom of the cup was still damp with the remains of what appears to be tea.

"The handkerchief was snuggly wrapped around the cup as you see it here. As I went through the car, I found an identical cup lying beneath one of the seats at the front of the car. This second cup was empty and nearly dry. The cups are probably identical to the ones your constable found on the other seats of the carriage."

"And where is the coat, Miss Davies?" asked the chief inspector.

"The coat was returned to Theda O'Neill."

"Thank you for bringing what you found, Miss Davies," said a solemn Chief

Inspector Lewis, "but I would have appreciated had you brought it in yesterday, including the coat."

"Ie, I understand, sir. The depot was chaotic, and we spent the remainder of the day and late into the evening in the lobby, calming waiting passengers and assisting your officers as they questioned everyone. It was very late before I remembered the cups in my satchel. We brought them in as soon as we could today." Drew kept her eyes locked onto the chief's, knowing full well she had told him a lie.

Chief Inspector Lewis nodded and then produced a box from under the counter, placed the two cups and the handkerchief inside, and walked around to where Drew and Howard were standing. Extending his hand to Howard, he said, "Always good to see you, Davies."

"Good to see you as well, Lewis, and it would be good to sit with a pint one evening and just catch up on anything other than business."

Lewis agreed as Granda and Drew departed the stationhouse.

"Do you think they'll find anything from the tests they hopefully run?" asked Drew as they climbed into the lorry.

"I trust Lewis to carefully oversee the process of any evidence presented to him. And ie, I would not be surprised if results of testing find the presence of a toxin in the dried remains of the cup, suggesting Miss Swan's death was not by natural causes. And I am supposing, Drew Girl, that you have a very good reason for not giving Miss Swan's coat to Chief Inspector Lewis?"

Drew nodded but gave no explanation as she settled the mustard-colored coat on her lap, a cacophony of questions and possibilities coursing through her mind. She needed to write down all that she wanted to do in the next few days, including the people she most wanted to speak with.

SORROW – TUESDAY, MARCH 25

Drew's morning at the depot was busy tamping down rumors and calming all the restless employees and concerned passengers. News travels fast, and the people buying tickets asked her a myriad of questions about "the woman found dead on the train." How did she die? Who found her? Was she murdered? And the most-asked question: Is it safe to travel on the train?

Earlier that morning, Chief Inspector Lewis and the railway executive had met with all the employees from the station, instructing them on how to answer such questions, including saying, "Of course, it is safe to travel on any of the trains."

Drew remained a bastion of calm throughout the day, a soothing smile set upon her face as she listened to the same inquiries dozens of times and gave the same reassuring response to each one. Granda talked with the newspapers but refused to allow pictures to be taken. One photographer, his large camara half exposed under his day coat, was able to make his way onto the platform but was stopped and nearly accosted by Jonesy, who grabbed him by the collar and loudly escorted him out the front entrance. The point seemed to be well-taken by the remainder of the newspapermen and their cameras. For once, Drew almost approved of Jonesy's high-handed methods.

It was past noon, and no one had paused for lunch. No trains were due again till three. "Granda, I want to drive over to the vicarage and make sure Liam and Theda are not being harassed as we are. May I take the lorry? I'll leave my bike here and be back by 2:30."

Howard had picked up a ringing phone halfway through Drew's request. He tossed her the keys, gave her a nod and a wave, and answered what was one more in a day of many calls.

With satchel and Eireann's coat in hand, Drew climbed into the lorry and was at the vicarage by half past noon. She found photographers, some the same ones that had been at the station, standing across the street from the house. A young constable, Officer Glendon Claerk, stood at attention outside the front gate. Drew was extremely happy to see him there, as he was always helpful and polite, at least initially.

"Good morning, Constable Claerk. My name is Drew Davies. We have met once or twice before. I am a friend of Vicar O'Neill and am returning a coat that belongs to his aunt."

"Yes, Miss Davies. My apologies, but the vicar has stated that they will not be receiving any visitors today. Perhaps tomorrow . . . or the day after. I can give him the coat if you like."

Drew had kept the coat, correctly assuming an officer would be at the house keeping everyone away from the vicarage's front door, especially the newspapers. She also assumed the constable would generously offer to return the coat.

"Ie, could you please go knock at the door, give them the coat, and let them know that Drew Davies is the one returning it? I'll wait here."

Officer Claerk looked across the road and saw the crowd was behaving itself, nodded to Drew, and proceeded up the front steps, giving a loud rap at the door. Drew watched as Liam opened the door and listened to the officer. He looked past the man and, seeing Drew, motioned for her to come up to the house. Officer Claerk nodded at Liam and stood aside as she made her way inside. Liam closed the door, putting a finger to his lips, and motioned for Drew to follow him into the kitchen.

"Aunt Theda is finally sleeping. We were both awake most of the night. Her tears ran all the way till morning. Let us hope she can rest a few hours. It is good to see you, Drew. I wanted to talk with you but didn't want to ring you at the depot and bother you on what must be a trying day there for all of you."

"What a relief to see the officer guarding your gate. There have been throngs of the curious at the depot all morning, as well as the newspaper types and their photographers. Two officers are there as well. The staff are carrying on as best they can.

"May I say again how terribly sorry I am, Liam. I want you to know that we will do everything we can to find out exactly what happened to your aunt. The railway company has investigators as well as the police seeking information, and Granda and I will be personally looking into what happened."

"Aunt Theda keeps telling me she knows that Eireann was murdered, that she worried for years that something like this would happen. She thought it would have been twenty years ago, though, not now, when their lives are without chaos. I don't understand what all that means, but she seems adamant to talk to the authorities about it."

Drew did not have a lot of faith in "the authorities" conducting a thorough investigation, as they had been less than thorough when Vicar Hughes was murdered. But then, the government had been involved, and perhaps without that element in this situation the local authorities might prove more effective in their efforts. In the meantime, given that she was an employee of the railway company, Drew felt that demanded some reasonable efforts on her own part to find out as much as she could. She was more than eager to talk with the other passengers from Ireland.

Hearing a rustling, they turned to the sitting room and saw Theda walking slowly toward them. She was wrapped in the extra blanket Drew had placed at the bottom of her bed, her hair mussed and her sad eyes red from tears of grief. Liam rose and went to her side. "Auntie, could you not sleep longer? It's only been an hour or so."

Theda swept her hand in a motion of dismissal and moved to an empty kitchen chair. "Miss Davies, I am so relieved to see you. Can you tell us any news? There have been no calls letting us know *anything*, including when we can see Eireann, and I really must go be with her."

The immense grief of these two people was palpable and spurred Drew to say, "Let me ring my grandfather and have him ring Chief Inspector Lewis. He'll find out where Eireann is and when you can go there." Drew went to the sitting room to make the phone call. It was the same phone on the same table she had used to ring the police when she found Vicar Hughes dead in his bedroom.

The line was busy on the first and second tries, but Drew persisted, and Granda answered on the third. She explained the situation and was assured he would ring Lewis immediately and ring them back at the vicarage. "Granda, I really feel I need to stay with Miss O'Neill and Liam for the remainder of this afternoon."

"I agree," said Granda. "We're coping well here. I'll ring you back shortly."

Drew returned to the kitchen. "Granda is ringing the constabulary and will find out what he can and ring us back. He and Chief Inspector Lewis served in the wars together and have a long-standing respect for one another. I know he'll find out what is happening. In the meantime, I am going to put the kettle on and make tea. And Miss O'Neill, while the water boils might I ask you a question or two?"

"Of course. I will answer anything I can. And please, call me Theda."

Twenty minutes and two cups of tea later, the phone rang. Liam suggested Drew answer it. Whether it be kind people from the congregation, nosey others, or Drew's grandfather, he asked that she take the call.

It was Granda, and he, as she knew he would, had some answers. "Miss Swan's body has been examined and will be released this morning, and after the certificate of death is signed, the body can be moved to a funeral home for arrangements. I realize Liam may not know where to have his aunt taken, so I am going to make a suggestion. Do you have paper and pen?"

Drew set down the phone and walked quickly to the kitchen, where she took paper and a pen from her satchel and returned to the sitting room. "Go ahead," she said, and wrote down the information. "If they want to have Eireann moved there, I will drive them to the hospital in the lorry and then to the funeral home. I'd like to stay with them as long as needed."

"You do that, Drew Girl, and we'll take care of things here. I will ride your bicycle home and see you when you get there. You are a fine young woman."

Drew ended the conversation with tears in her eyes and wiped them away quickly before returning to Liam and Theda. "Eireann's body has been released from the authorities. The medical examiner just needs to sign the paperwork to move her from the hospital to a funeral home. Granda gave me the number of a reputable one here in Mumbles. If you agree, we need to ring them and see how soon they can meet you at the hospital. If it would be helpful, I can drive you there to be with Eireann when she is moved." Drew paused as she took in their sorrowful faces. "I am more than sorry that this is all happening."

"Did the inspector tell your grandfather the cause of death?" asked Liam.

"He didn't say and I didn't ask," responded Drew.

"We'll need to talk with the medical examiner when we get to the hospital, or whoever signed the document releasing Eireann to us."

Theda stared out the windows into the back yard as Liam reached for the slip of paper on which Drew had written the name and number of the funeral home. He motioned toward his aunt, and Drew nodded that she would stay with her as he got up to make the call. Theda grabbed Drew's hand and held on for dear life as they listened to Liam's sad litany of information.

"The funeral director said he would personally meet us at the hospital in an hour and did we want to go back to the funeral home and talk with him about any arrangements. I told him we probably would but may not know exactly what those arrangements would be at this time."

Theda slowly nodded her head and patted Drew's hand, saying, "I will be ready to leave in fifteen minutes."

Liam said he needed to ready himself as well and thought he would wear his vestiges of the clergy, as he felt both aunts would greatly appreciate it. Drew sat at the table and composed herself for what was most likely an afternoon of difficult decisions.

Arriving at the hospital to sign the documents and take possession of the body, they were met by an officer who had been stationed with Eireann's body, awaiting the family's arrival. He informed Theda that she was to remain in Wales until such a time that the police had an opportunity to speak with her again. They had additional questions that needed answers. Theda merely nodded. But Drew realized that Eireann's body would not be able to leave Wales until the police also released Theda to return home.

Drew stepped into the hallway and looked round until she saw someone who appeared to be in charge. "Is the medical examiner available to talk with us regarding his findings?" she asked. "The family would like to speak with him or someone in authority before they leave."

The employee said he did not know but would inquire, and they could continue to wait with the body. Several minutes later, a large man wearing enormous round spectacles entered the room, his long white medical coat billowing about his body as if he had wings.

"Dr. John Powell, medical examiner," he said with a brief nod. "I have only a few minutes but am happy to answer your questions. What is it you would like to know? I have just this morning spoken to Chief Inspector Lewis about my findings."

Liam stepped toward the man, extending his hand and saying, "Thank you for speaking with us. I am Vicar Liam O'Neill, Miss Swan's nephew. Before the funeral director arrives, we would appreciate it if you could also tell us what you found. Specifically, how did my aunt die?"

"Well, it is quite disturbing, really. The presence of digitalis was found in Miss Swan's system. Digitalis is lethal and fast acting. There are no marks of any sort on the body, which led me to the conclusion that the cause of death was heart failure as a result of ingesting the digitalis. As I said, the police have been sent my report, and I assume they will be contacting you shortly as they proceed with their investigation. I am very sorry for your loss." Dr. Powell handed Liam the signed certificate of death, turned, and left the room as quickly as he had flown in.

All was quiet as Theda stood between the supporting arms of Liam and Drew. "I knew they would find it was not from natural causes. But why? Why now, after all these years?" Sobbing, Theda turned to Liam and fell into his arms.

The hearse from the funeral home arrived some minutes later, and two men swiftly placed the body inside. Drew, Liam, and Theda followed the long black car to the home, and after the difficult decisions had been made, Drew drove Liam and Theda back to the vicarage.

She pulled the lorry up to the front gate and stopped. "Before you both go inside, I want to tell you that I am fairly certain of how Eireann was poisoned. After the authorities removed her body from the train carriage and the constables left the car as well, I went back inside. That is when I found Eireann's coat—still on her seat. I admit, I was looking for anything the police overlooked or hadn't yet seen. I was surprised they had left her coat, but they may have assumed it was yours, Theda.

"I thoroughly searched the seats you had occupied, and in picking up the coat, I went through the pockets. That is when I found a teacup wrapped in what I assumed was Eireann's large handkerchief. The linen was damp with what I believe were the remnants of tea. Theda, can you confirm once more that you had tea before you arrived at the station?"

"Yes, yes. A gentleman from the dining carriage came through with a tray of tea already poured, asking if we would like one before arriving at the station. We were both delighted and thought that was a kind gesture on the part of the railway. As you know, after I finished my tea I used the lavatory, and by the time I returned to our seats, my Eireann was gone." Theda's eyes filled with tears again but also with resignation. "Do you suspect there was poison in the tea?"

"Ie, I believe there was. When I found the cup and linen, I went through the rest of the car, examining every seat, under the seats, and in the above racks. In addition to the cups the constable found, I found one more cup under a seat at the front of the car. The cups are identical, with a green stamp on the bottom that was at first difficult to make out. I do know they are not Great Western inventory nor used in the dining cars. And the brand mark indicates the cups were manufactured in Ireland.

"Yesterday, Granda and I took both cups and the handkerchief to the constabulary and gave them to Chief Inspector Lewis, hoping they could find fingerprints and test what was left in the cup and on the cloth. Have they spoken to you about tea being served on the train?"

"No, we spoke only briefly on the train and then for a few minutes after her body was taken away by the ambulance. Their questions seemed cursory at best, as though they had done their due diligence and we could be on our way. They did say they wanted to speak further at some point, as the officer said again at the hospital just now."

The three of them sat in silence for some minutes before Liam bid Drew good night and escorted his aunt inside the house.

Drew arrived home late that evening, having supported Liam and Theda as best she could, both at the hospital and at the funeral home. She had listened silently as the bereft aunt and nephew, aided by gentle guidance from the funeral director, made the decision to have Eireann cremated and her ashes placed in an urn that they chose. The funeral home would let them know when the urn would be ready for Theda to take into her possession.

Drew wondered if Chief Inspector Lewis and the experts examining the teacups and the linen had made any headway. She fully expected them to find traces of digitalis and hopefully fingerprints that would corroborate the medical examiner's findings and lead them to the murderer.

In her bed that evening, with Vesuvi close by her side, Drew went over all the events of the day, making additional notes and adding to her list of questions. There was much to do.

CHAPTER 12

JONESY – WEDNESDAY, MARCH 26

"What's this I'm hearing, Davies? The men are telling me some nonsense about your girl wanting the guard job. I told 'em I'd come straight away to see you, and you'd be quick to call it nonsense as well."

"Good day to you too, Jonesy. You heard it the same as me. And Drew is not 'my girl.' She is an employee of the railway company the same as we all are, and if qualified, she can apply for the job."

"I told you my nephew wants the job. You know that because I asked your girl if she would help him with some understanding in *The Book of Rules* about signaling. And don't tell me you don't remember *that*, Davies!"

Jonesy had stormed into the office as though Drew was not sitting at her desk and it was just himself and the station master present. Drew had expected word to get out that she, indeed, was applying for the job, and she also expected Jonesy to act out in protest. She had played this scene over in her mind many times before this morning and was glad to have it here and over with today.

She rose purposefully from her desk, head held high, and walked her tall frame to stand in front of Jonesy, looking down in an attempt to meet his eyes. "Did you not notice I was in the room, Jonesy? It sounds like it's me you need to be talking to, since I'm the one applying for the job."

Jonesy's agitation was rising. "You *cannot* work as a train guard. What gives you any idea you can do that job?"

"Are you familiar with the qualifications needed? I meet them all, including already being a railway employee, as well as someone from a railroading family. Tell me, Jonesy, how is your nephew any more qualified than I am, especially since he doesn't even work for the company, and, from what I hear, has no experience around trains at all?"

"You're not qualified because you are a female! It's not natural for a female to be out there in the yard on the tracks and around the trains. The work is too hard. And it takes a special understanding to do the job!"

"What special understanding is it specifically that is required that isn't listed in the job description? As far as I read, I meet all the requirements and more."

"See! Right there! That's the reason females can't do this work. You don't understand what it really takes because females aren't logical. Not logical or mechanical to be able to do this work."

"Have you forgotten, Jonesy, that during the war hundreds of women worked railway positions all across Britain? And the women were good at what they did. Many didn't want to leave those jobs when the men returned, but they had no choice. Well, the war is over now, and when jobs open up, as long as the person, male or female, is qualified, they can apply for the job. And no, I won't be helping your nephew when it comes to understanding signaling. Being a man, and therefore so logical, surely he can figure it out for himself."

Drew turned away from the irrational, rude man and walked slowly back to the front of her desk, leaning against the hard surface of it, never taking her eyes off him.

Barely controlling his rage, Jonesy kept his steady gaze on Howard, never once looking at Drew. "This isn't the natural way of things, Davies, and you *know* it! This isn't the last you'll be hearing from me *and* the other men." He stormed out of the office, leaving behind the sweaty stench of anger and frustration.

Drew took her seat behind her desk and picked up her pen to record the ticket sales from the last train departure. The fire burning in her soul and the slight tremor in her hands fueled her determination. She would complete the job application for the van guard position today. Jonesy and all the men could take their discontent and swagger all the way home to complain to their "illogical" women.

CHAPTER 13

ALWAYS THE LIGHT – THURSDAY, MARCH 27

Rex Archer was focused intently on the panoramic view of Bristol Bay laid out before him. Arriving on the train merely three days before, he and his family had taken rooms at Mrs. Stable's Bed and Breakfast. Following the death of a passenger and the subsequent questioning of every passenger on the train by the police constables, Rex was informed that he and his family were to remain close at hand until the authorities finished their inquiries.

He had planned this trip to Wales some time ago and had already reserved lodging for a month in the beautiful seaside village of Mumbles. A self-proclaimed plein-air painter, the last two mornings saw Rex rising shortly after dawn to set up his tripod easel, side table, and stool. He arranged his palette, brushes, tubes of oils, palette knife, a container of mineral spirits, and a few small rags in precisely the same positions each morning. He did not wear his snappy green beret, although he would have liked to. But his wife, Eva, refused to allow it. She said he looked like "a foolish impostor." However, he always wore his color-stained painter's coat—wore it with pride, for it was colorful evidence of his efforts and ambition.

"Good morning, Mr. Archer!" called Drew as she approached the man.

"Oh my! You startled me, young woman. Never approach a painter, especially one as focused as myself, when we are deep into our creative space. Just isn't good form, you know." Rex Archer spoke with a strong Irish lilt, his voice sounding almost musical as it carried across the morning's breeze.

Drew walked a few steps toward the easel, taking in the tall, exceptionally slender man. His thinning pale red hair was moving about in the wind, and as he turned toward her, she saw his eyes were a startling green. "I sincerely apologize. I certainly hope I didn't cause your brush to go astray."

"Well, oils are very unforgiving, and you are fortunate that I was painting in my mind's eye the moment you approached, therefore, no harm was done. I believe I saw you at the station just after that terrible sequence of events. The poor woman. Do the police have any idea what could have caused her death?"

"I don't believe the authorities have released any information to the public. At least, that is my understanding. As an employee of the railway, I have been speaking with passengers on the train that arrived with Miss Swan's body, asking if anyone observed anything or anyone out of the ordinary."

"As a painter, Miss Davies, I am constantly observing my surroundings, aware and attuned to all I see and hear. I neither saw nor heard anything unusual, only the typical bustle of railway employees moving about the carriages, attending to passengers as the train rumbled along."

"Were you seated with your family during the journey?"

"My wife and children sit where they choose. They know I am watching the views from the window and ruminating on my art and do not like to be disturbed. So no, I did not sit with my wife and children, and other than using the toilet and purchasing food, I did not leave my seat but was entirely focused on my sketchbook."

Well, so much for Mr. Archer being constantly "attuned" to his surroundings, thought Drew. In the picture he painted of himself, Rex Archer posed no threat to Eireann Swan. He seemed completely self-absorbed. But Drew knew people could present themselves in whatever light they chose, and this plein-air painter could be creating a false impression of naive innocence.

Rex turned back to his easel, making short brushstrokes of bright blue. "Well, I know the police have it all well in hand and not to worry. I am quite content to stay as long as they say we must. This is the perfect picturesque village for a serious painter to hone his craft. While my wife, an avid city aficionado, does not relish remaining here in the least, a month in such a small seaside community was my intent and purpose for our travels, and I am enjoying every opportunity to paint."

"Ie, I am sure you are. And what type of painting is it that you do, Mr. Archer? What style, I mean?"

"Impressionism is my preferred style. Usually executed plein-air, out of doors, you see, where the air is fresh, the light pure, and the colors are most vibrant."

Drew moved her head this way and that, attempting to make sense of the half-finished canvas. "Are you hoping to capture a picture of the water and landscape in front of you? Again, I apologize, I know nothing of painting and certainly nothing about impressionism."

"Have you heard, Miss . . . what is your name again?"

"Drew. Drew Davies."

"Miss Davies. Are you at all familiar with the great impressionist artists such as Monet, Renoir, and Pissarro? They are wonderful examples of what I, myself, am striving to create: to capture the *essence* of what we see before us. The *spirit* of what inspires us to put paint to canvas."

"Ah, I think I understand. It is not intended to look like what you actually see, so to speak."

Rex turned to look quizzically at Drew. "It is rather hard to explain to someone not at all versed in the language of art. You are not an artist. You cannot be expected to see the world with the eyes of an experienced painter such as myself. But do not berate yourself, few have the gift, you know. Now, I must bid you goodbye and get back to it before I lose the light."

"Thank you, Mr. Archer. I very much enjoyed our chat. Before I leave, can you please tell me where I might find your wife and children today?"

"I believe Eva said they were going down to the strand, but I have no idea where that might be. But do come again, Miss Davies, if you would like to observe and learn. Just please, do not creep up on me."

Drew couldn't help smiling before saying, "Next time, I will make a gentler approach. And just one more question, Mr. Archer. What was your purpose again in coming to Wales?"

Rex Archer turned to Drew, an incredulous look on his face, and said, "Because of the light! Always the light, Miss Davies!"

Drew took her leave and turned to the entrance of the bed and breakfast, where she found Mrs. Maggie Stables standing behind her front desk sorting mail. The woman had been the perpetual and sole proprietor of the Stables B and B long before Drew made her entrance into the world. Although she went by "missus," no one had ever seen the "mister." Maggie Stables ran her business with an intensity bordering on rudeness . . . and sometimes just plain rudeness. Drew, being a bit afraid of the short, stout woman with an aura of swirling dark green, knew better than to speak a "hello" and instead stood in silence. She certainly did not want to "startle" another person hard at work.

"I can see you there, Miss Davies. Say what you must, I've not got all day."

"*Bore da*, Mrs. Stables. I don't mean to interrupt you. I merely came by to drop off mail that arrived at our cottage by mistake."

"Would you not think the mail could at least arrive at the right place to the right people at the right time? How many times has this happened now? I do not expect an answer, Miss Davies, so you can close your mouth. Leave my mail on the desk and depart."

With a smile, Drew set the two envelopes on top of the long wooden counter and headed to the door before turning toward Mrs. Stables and asking, "Are you enjoying your guests from Ireland? Do they seem a happy family enjoying their time in our village?"

The innkeeper paused and looked at Drew. "It is always interesting to have out-of-country guests—though some are more congenial than others. And as to whether they are a 'happy' family or a miserable lot is neither your business nor mine. I do know they came in on the train with the dead woman, but I see nothing of conspiracy about them."

"What do you see Mrs. Stables?"

"Nothing other than a pompous man, a contentious woman, and two lonely children. Now be on your way, Drew Davies.

She stood outside on the grass for several minutes, watching Mr. Archer. Try as she might, she could not see the least bit of resemblance to what was splayed on his canvas to the view of the water and waves before him. He had caught sight of her as she walked to her bicycle and called out, "Come again, Miss Davies! I welcome you to observe my process whenever you are inclined."

She gave the man a wave, saying, "Thank you, Mr. Archer. I may just do that."

However, it wasn't Mr. Archer's process she had come to observe today, and would possibly again, but the man himself. How fortunate mail intended for Mrs. Stables just happened to end up in Drew's hands when she went by the post office to visit her friend Joanne, the postmistress.

CHAPTER 14

A TALE OF WOE – THURSDAY, MARCH 27

Drew walked the shifting sand down to the water, where she thought Eva Archer and the children might be found. The wind was waning, just a gentle breeze teasing the promise of an early spring. There was only one person on the beach, and Drew presumed this was Mrs. Archer.

The woman had flung a blanket across the sand whereupon she set two chairs. She was sitting on one with a straw hat pulled tightly onto her head and a thick woven scarf wrapped around the collar of an even thicker sweater. While it was apparent the woman was not falling for a false promise of a spring day, the children seemed to think otherwise. They were in their swimming attire and, as the water caressed the shore, were wildly playing catch with the waves.

"Good day, Mrs. Archer. My name is Drew Davies, from the railway station. I hope I am not intruding upon your day, but I was wondering if you might do me a favor. One that does not require you leaving your seat in the sun."

"Hello, Miss Davies. I expected someone from the rail company to show up sooner or later. And I have been waiting to hear from the police again, but no sign of them either. You are a welcome sight, as I have been rather bored by all this quaint village scenery and have hardly spoken to anyone other than the librarians. Thank God for your library! Although my husband and children are having a fine time of it, I am ready to be on our way home by way of London. So please," she said, patting the chair next to her, "sit and tell me what you might require."

Drew settled herself on the folding chair. "I told my grandmother that you were a passenger on the train and staying at Mrs. Stable's. She shared that she was a great fan of yours, has followed your career, and was wondering if you might autograph an article she had kept."

"A fan, all this way from civilization? That will certainly make this day more pleasurable."

"I have the article here with me, and I've brought a pen. I took the liberty of reading the column, and I must say, you are quite famous. And here you are in our little village."

Drew reached for one of several magazines Mrs. Archer had stacked on her blanket. She placed the newspaper clipping on top and along with her fountain pen handed both to Mrs. Archer.

Eva read through the article, smiled, and signed the middle of it, saying quietly, "Well, unfortunately, that was one of my last performances on a London stage. It could have been only the beginning, but no matter how I cajoled and pleaded, my husband, Rex, insisted we go back to Belfast so he could attend to his business. He was not about to leave me and the children alone in London, fearing I might spend all of his fortune. If only I had it to do over again," she mused with a faraway look. "London was always my true home."

She sighed with regret as she capped the pen and handed it back to Drew along with the signed article. Placing the back of one hand and forearm across her brow, Eva laid her head back against the chair, looking as forlorn as a lovely woman on the beach could possibly be.

"You are from Ireland, correct? I ask because you do not sound Irish; your speech is very British."

"Rex and I both attended boarding schools in London. Mine was a school for young women in the very heart of the city, where my own heart will always be. As far as my accent is concerned, I worked hard to leave all vestiges of being

Irish behind me when I went away to school. I decided early on that I would speak the Queen's English, while Rex fiercely held onto his brogue."

"Why couldn't you perform on stage in Ireland? I'm sure you would have had great success wherever you were."

"London is the only true stage worthy of great performances. There is nothing in miserable Ireland that holds a candle to what I could still achieve in England. But Mr. Archer is a peevish and uncharitable man. A selfish husband who has been coddled and pampered all his life. He is the only child of a man who made millions investing in the rubber plantations in the colonies and left his millions to his miserly son. Because he holds the purse strings and still dabbles in the family business, Belfast is where we live."

"What a difficult circumstance for a woman to find herself in. For her life to be solely orchestrated by her husband. I'm surprised, since Mr. Archer is himself an artist, that he is not more sensitive to your endeavors as well."

Giving Drew a sidelong glance with eyebrows raised, Eva said, "Well dear, you are young and do not understand the ways of the world, which is the world according to men who control everything and therefore have all the power. Once we had the children, my career was virtually over, and I was subjugated to the life of a rich, bored woman."

"How long did you live in London? Do you ever visit?"

"Children! Do not go any farther into the water than your knees!" shouted Mrs. Archer abruptly. "I'll have to take them in soon, as they will freeze their feet off. To answer your question, we met and married in Belfast, went on an extended world excursion for our honeymoon, and ended up in London for many blissful years. I never wanted to leave. Ireland seemed to be constantly at war with itself, and the incessant fighting made living there untenable at best. London was so alive and vibrant, and I found success on the stage at every turn.

"Every year, including this one, and especially now that the war is over, I propose we take a second home in the English countryside. After all, the children will soon be in a fine boarding school in London, and since he travels so much on business, what difference would it make to him where we lived." Mrs. Archer had sat upright, looking intently at Drew as she spoke. Strands of dark hair had eluded the confines of her hat and blew about her face, her chocolate-brown eyes both intense and sorrowful. Then she sat back and stared out to the water, seemingly far away in London, her thoughts focusing on what could have been.

Wanting to keep her talking, Drew said, "And obviously it does make a difference to him where you live."

"Obviously, and now he wants to drag us with him from country to country, seeking out 'the perfect light, the perfect coastline,' so he can sit by the water and play the artist while I chase the children about and think evil thoughts of him."

Mrs. Archer turned to face Drew. "You must think I am a terrible person, a most officious wife and neglectful mother. But I will do anything and go anywhere to keep my children in good health and ensure they have a good life, so really, why can I not do that in London and have my career as well? Rex cannot see past his own egocentric nose. He is no more an artist than my children are swimmers. Really, life is merely a study in regret and disappointment."

She stood up suddenly, her long legs attempting to find balance on the blanket, and yelled, "Children! If I have to say it one more time, we are going inside for the day!"

What she didn't say is that, as Rex Archer's wife, she was amply provided for as well as the children. Supposedly, as long as she played the part of the dutiful, supportive wife and mother, she could live a lavish lifestyle, albeit not in London. Drew wondered how many countless women suffered the same stagnation in a marriage, where the wife had no money and therefore no power and few options, unable to make choices and decisions for themselves and their family. It was a situation she vowed she would never find herself in. "Do you have family in Belfast? Your parents and siblings, perhaps, for company?"

"My family died some time ago, and I, like Rex, have no siblings."

"So, what do you do to keep yourself occupied? Do you ever act in theatrical groups?"

"Yes, I do act from time to time and even wanted to start my own local theatre company, where I could give classes and have other actors come to learn in workshops I would teach. We would put on plays and productions, and it could be wonderful. But you can imagine how that proposal failed when I approached Rex with the idea. It was too 'common' a thing for a person of our social class to be involved in such work. 'Crass,' I believe he called the idea."

Drew found herself quite disgusted with Rex Archer. What a brute of a husband! She would never have a relationship with such a man.

"I am sincerely sorry for your unhappiness, Mrs. Archer. Thank goodness you have your children—"

"Well, they are of little company and will soon be off as well," interrupted Eva. "And then what am I to do with myself? Once we leave this place, I may just need to stand my ground and take myself and the children to London for the summer."

Drew was quiet for some time, letting space offer some solace before a change of subject. "Mrs. Archer, I am here for another reason besides your coveted autograph. As an employee of the railway, I am talking with everyone who was on the train the day the woman died. May I ask you the same questions I just asked your husband?"

"Of course, Miss Davies. I have all the languid time in the world. Ask on."

"Can you tell me what carriage you and your children were seated in during the train trip?"

"We were one car ahead of Rex, although I don't know the number of the carriage, only that he was behind us and there were more cars ahead."

"Did you see anyone or anything that would seem out of the ordinary?"

Mrs. Archer squinted her face, lowered her sunglasses, and asked, "What would that have looked like, 'out of the ordinary' I mean? Can you give me an example?"

"Well, as an actress yourself, you would be in a position to notice if someone was behaving suspiciously or out of character, perhaps."

"I am sorry, but most of the trip I was attempting to play a card game with my unruly children, when all they wanted to do was run up and down the aisle, pestering the other passengers. I was quite embarrassed when the conductor asked them twice to sit in their seats and then came to me insisting I make them behave. Really, I do not know what the man expected me to do! I will be quite relieved when they are off to school come fall. Rex assures me the boarding school will make them into fine young persons, just as they did us." At this, Eva removed her very large sunglasses, rolled her eyes, and reached into her bag for her pack of cigarettes and a book of matches.

Drew waited patiently until the woman lit the cigarette and had blown smoke above her head before asking, "So to clarify, Mrs. Archer, you did not observe anything you might construe as unusual?"

"That is correct, Miss Davies."

"Did you ever leave the car during the train ride?"

"I left my seat to use the lavatory and to go to the dining car. Do you have children, Miss Davies? Of course, you don't, you are a 'miss.' Well, let me tell you that when you do, they will demand to be fed constantly, from the time they are born until . . . well, who knows till when? I hardly eat, so it is hard for me to understand their obsession with food." Eva continued blowing smoke and watching her children.

"Well, thank you for your time, Mrs. Archer. Perhaps we will meet again before you leave. I have enjoyed talking with you."

"Yes, yes. It is always nice to meet a fan. Good day, Miss Davies."

Drew didn't quite know what to make of the woman or her tale of woe. Mrs. Eva Archer did not seem the type of woman to let anyone thwart her passions, and yet she would have you believe she was at the mercy of a selfish, egocentric, controlling husband. Perhaps, thought Drew, this was another one of her great performances.

CHAPTER 15

MEETING MR. BENNETT – THURSDAY, MARCH 27 AND FRIDAY, MARCH 28

When Drew arrived back at the station, after her curious conversations with the Archers, there was a long queue of passengers formed to purchase tickets. She hurried to open the ticket window and greeted them all as calmly as she could while her mind whirred away. It was hectic until five o'clock, when the last passengers of the day purchased their tickets for the later train and the office staff prepared to go home.

There had been no time to talk with Granda about the two hours she had spent interviewing Mr. and Mrs. Archer, and she was eager to tell him all about it.

Once home, the two sat at the kitchen table as Nonna prepared dinner. After talking with the Archers, Drew had again scribbled notes on more stray slips of paper between her tasks at the depot. She now pulled days' worth of notes from her satchel and laid them all on the table, trying to smooth out the wrinkles and put them in order.

Howard shook his head and kept a smile on his face as he listened to her piece together the threads of the conversations from the wrinkled collection.

"And that is all they told me: that neither left their respective train carriages other than to use the facilities and buy food. And both said they saw nothing out of the ordinary, but then, how would they know, as they were both enmeshed in their own concerns. At least that is what they said."

"They certainly seem like two interesting characters! And did you get any chance to visit with their children?"

"No, but Charlotte and Lillian tell me their mother brings them to the library most days around noon to choose a book and sit for an hour or two reading before they go for tea. I plan to happen by one day next week to return my own books and hopefully have a chance to talk again. Charlotte tells me the daughter is about eleven and the boy a few years younger.

"Tomorrow after work I am going to talk with Mr. William Bennett, who was in the same carriage with Eireann and Theda. He also was the first to respond to Theda's cries for help. I got his address from Joanne. She said when he arrived on the train from Ireland, he took possession of a cottage he purchased not far from ours and plans to settle permanently in Mumbles."

"You have been busy, Drew Girl! A regular sleuth in search of information. I would, however, suggest that you find a more efficient and professional manner in which to organize your notes."

Granda reached under his chair and placed a wrapped package in front of her. Nonna turned round with a smile on her face, wiping her hands on her apron.

"And what is this? A surprise? You both know I am not one for surprises, but . . ." Drew quickly tore off the blue paper and found a notebook, a leather-bound journal with beautiful gilded edges. The book was smaller than her novels, the size perfect for her satchel. She leafed through its creamy blank pages, then reached into her satchel again and pulled out her fountain pen, one left to her from her mother's collection. She carefully signed her name and date to the front page.

"Right after dinner I will transfer all my notes into this lovely and much-needed gift. No more scrounging for bits and pieces of stray paper to write on.

Thank you both so much!" Drew rose and gave them tight hugs. She put the pen and journal back in her satchel and then helped Nonna put dinner on the table.

True to her word, that night she took the journal to bed. She began by adding all of her notes from the train affair: the day Eireann was found dead, finding the woman's coat and the teacups, her talks with Liam and Theda, and lastly, her interviews today with the Archers. She was eagerly looking forward to talking with Mr. Bennett tomorrow.

Drew arranged with Granda to go to work later than usual, allowing her to meet with Mr. Bennett first thing. Annebelle had proved surprisingly capable of fulfilling some of Drew's responsibilities when she was out of the station.

As Drew approached Mr. Bennett's home, she slowed her bicycle, taking a long look at the cottage set far back from the road. It was in obvious need of repairs. That was putting it kindly, as everything about the house was in a sad state of affairs. The roof was drooping, several shingles hung askew, and the front door needed at least a coat or two of paint. But aside from what the house lacked, the many trees, shrubs, and Welsh ferns in the yard were lovely. Beautiful garden beds abounded around the cottage, with early spring flowers just beginning to grace the generous spaces. The lavish gardens made the cottage a fairy tale house that just needed some dust from those fairies to put it all to rights again.

Drew was enthralled. It did not appear to be inhabited, and for a moment she wondered if this was truly the correct address. Then she saw smoke curl slowly above the chimney and knew someone was at home. As she approached the front door, she also thought she smelled toast and was instantly wishing she had taken time to have her breakfast.

Laying her bike gently on the ground, she slung her leather satchel over her shoulder, her new journal tucked safely inside, and walked toward the door. Vines of unruly wisteria meandered their way along the walls on both sides of and above the entry. She knew it would be a beautiful sight when they were in bloom. The door opened abruptly before she could lift her hand to knock.

"Good morning, young lady. Might I assist you?"

The first thing she noticed about the man standing before her was that he wore a monocle. She had read of characters wearing them in her beloved mystery books but had never actually seen anyone wear such an eyepiece. This somehow gave her the impression that he was well acquainted with his and perhaps enjoyed the idea of wearing a monocle as much he enjoyed the improved vision it provided. It suited his person so perfectly.

The second thing she noticed was he probably wasn't as old as he appeared at first glance. A thick dressing gown of brown wool was tied tight to his wide waist, and the slippers on his feet looked well worn and cozy. Drew thought he must be in his late fifties or so, with a full head of mussed wavy white hair highlighting his deep blue eyes. Warm air drifted from the door, as did the scent of something delicious, and she hoped he was about to invite her in.

"Miss? Are you alright?"

"Oh, I am sorry. Ie, I am fine and hoping that you are Mr. William Bennett. My name is Drew Davies. I am an employee of the Great Western Line and conducting a series of interviews with the passengers who were on the train when Miss Eireann Swan died. I am hoping that I might have a word with you."

"You are certainly out early on your mission, but if you don't mind having a cuppa with me, you are welcome to come in and ask your questions. I was just sitting down to my meager breakfast, wondering what the day might bring, and here you are." He stood aside and waved one arm, welcoming her into his home.

Inside, she found it laid out almost exactly as her own cottage. A fire burned in the large kitchen hearth and the gentleman, for that is certainly what he seemed, did indeed have his table set.

"Please, take off your coat and have a seat. Would you be interested in tea and toast?"

"Ie, that sounds wonderful, as I've left home without my own breakfast this morning. As you say, it is early, and perhaps I should have sought you out later in the day. We live close by, but I didn't realize how close, that it would take me only minutes to arrive at your door. I do apologize for what now seems a rude hour to disturb you."

"Nonsense. I don't live by the clock, and most often I hardly know the day, much less the time. I'm glad you came, as I do want to meet my neighbors at some point, and today seems a good time to begin. Now, Miss Davies, sit and tell me how I may help you."

Drew took the chair offered and put her new journal and pen in front of her, opening it to a blank page ready for information.

Mr. Bennett placed a cup and saucer to her side. After warming the pot before filling it again and adding the tea to steep, he poured a heavenly fragrance into the cup. A small pitcher of milk and a sugar bowl were already on the table. He then made up two plates with thick toasted bread and slices of cheese and set them on the table for Drew and himself.

"Thank you, Mr. Bennett. I certainly did not expect to be warmed and fed. Your home is very familiar to me, as it is much like my own and has caught me somewhat off guard in its familiarity. I feel as though I have come to visit an old friend." Drew realized, stopping mid-air with her toast in hand, how that must sound so odd to him, as it certainly did to her. She was here as a professional, and she wasn't sounding or behaving as such.

Mr. Bennett smiled and chuckled softly, removing his monocle to wipe his eyes. Drew smiled as well, though not quite sure why, and they proceeded to eat what she found to be a welcome breakfast.

On to her second piece of toast, Drew asked, "How did you come to be here in this particular cottage? It appears to have been long unused."

"That is true. The estate agent told me it had not been lived in since before the war, and the family was quietly wanting to sell. I purchased it last month, and after settling my affairs in Ireland, I arrived on the train to move into my new life. Thus far, although it has only been a short while, it has proved all I hoped it would be: quiet and peaceful. I still must take delivery of more boxes, as they have not all arrived, but I have everything I need. The previous owners left the entire cottage intact: furniture, linens, dishes, all of it. The agent said their circumstances, something to do with the war, caused them to leave quickly. While sorry for their circumstances, I am grateful to have found such a lovely place.

"I hope to find a local carpenter to help me make repairs and set it all to rights. And the gardens I will tend to myself. They make up now for what the house lacks, don't they? But all will be restored in good time. I have both the time and the inclination."

As Drew finished her breakfast, she enjoyed listening to the man's accent. It was rather mesmerizing, and she was hoping that Mr. Bennett would refill their cups. She stopped herself just as she was about to ask him details of what he planned to do to the house. Instead, she said, "Might I ask why you left Ireland? And do you have family that will be joining you?"

"Belfast is a noisy and calamitous place, and I wanted to be somewhere in the quiet. I fear the country will forever be warring with itself. I cannot help the situation, and the memories of my life there wear on my soul. I am a writer, and we tend to be solitary by nature. I have always fancied myself practicing my craft in a quieter haven, such as this, and now was the perfect time to make the move.

"And yes, I have a daughter, Eileen, who will join me on occasion at some point. She is looking for a position, probably in Swansea. She is a physician and hoping to join a group of like-minded doctors close by. That is, if such an opportunity presents itself. She is looking into the possibilities. More tea, Miss Davies?"

Drew nodded eagerly as she continued taking notes, then asked, "I have been speaking with other passengers that were on the train when Eireann Swan died, and I would like to ask you similiar questions regarding the journey. What carriage were you in, and where did you sit?"

"I was in the same one as the woman who died. I sat four or five rows ahead on the same side. I didn't notice the two women until I heard the commotion and screams for help as we approached the depot. I jumped out of my seat, as did the few others in the carriage. As I approached them, one appeared unconscious, and the other was beside herself, pleading for help. I took the unconscious woman's pulse, could not find one, and then laid her down across the seats. I'd thought she had most likely fainted, but it was distressing not to find a heartbeat.

"By that time, the conductor arrived and instructed everyone to return to their seats, we were pulling into the depot. I made to return to my seat as he attempted to calm down the sobbing woman, telling her that as soon as the train stopped an ambulance would be called. I saw her kneeling by her friend as she continued to cry softly. I prayed I was wrong, that she had not died, that perhaps the woman had merely fainted, and I just could not detect her pulse."

"What happened when the train stopped at the station?"

Mr. Bennett rose, put more water in the kettle, and placed it on the burner before answering. "As the conductor said he would do, he jumped from the slowing train and ran into the depot. I moved toward the women again, a witness to the sorrow spilling from the sobbing woman's eyes. I stayed with her, with such a helpless feeling.

"I assumed the call was made to the authorities, as shortly thereafter an ambulance arrived as well as several constables. We were all directed to leave the train and find seats in the station lobby and to remain there. We were not to leave the depot under any circumstances. I believe the station master was the one directing us, and I realize now that you were there as well, helping escort people into the building. I saw the station master lock the entrance doors and positioned myself at a window looking out onto the tracks. When I did not see the woman immediately moved into the ambulance, I knew that most likely she had passed."

Mr. Bennett stopped talking, drank the remainder of his tea, and sighed heavily. Then he placed both palms on the table, pushed himself up, and refilled the teapot from the steaming kettle.

Drew sat quietly waiting for him to go on, pen poised in the air. When he sat again, he was quiet, gazing off as though reliving that day.

"What happened after that, Mr. Bennett? Did the police come speak to everyone?"

"Yes. Two constables came in and took all our names, addresses, and, if we had them, phone numbers of where we were staying.

"How many passengers do you estimate were in the lobby? How did they appear?"

"Not many. Perhaps twenty-five. Most were quiet and restrained. Some went to use the lavatories and returned. There was a young family with two small children that were restless and cried from time to time. There was another family, the father sounded Irish, and they had two older children. The police seemed to know most of the people, as they must have been residents, and they were allowed to leave quite soon. Several men in business attire must have been familiar as well, for they too were briefly questioned and allowed to go. The rest of us, who I assumed were not from the area, spent some time being questioned by the police. Many of the questions you are asking again now."

"I am sorry that I'm asking you to revisit that day. It must have been quite distressing. It certainly was for us, as employees of the railway."

"Yes, death is always disturbing, even if the person is not someone you know. Can you tell me who the woman was? I haven't seen anything in the papers about it."

"She was traveling with her companion, who is the aunt of the new vicar of the Anglican church in Oystermouth. They had come to visit for Easter and hear his first sermon. The police have not released any details of the death, as it is under investigation. The railway company obviously wants to find out as much information as possible to help find answers."

"Might I assume that foul play may have been involved and that is why we have heard nothing?"

"I really cannot say, but I would like to ask if you saw anything that appeared out of the ordinary occurring in your train car. Did anyone come in or go out of the carriage who seemed out of place or in any way distressed or nervous or angry?"

"I have thought about that over and over. The constable asked me that as well. I have traveled by rail often over the years and am familiar with the cast of personnel who work the trains. I saw no one leave or enter that car that wasn't an employee."

"Or at least they all appeared to be railway employees, Mr. Bennett. Were you offered a cup of tea just before the train approached Swansea, and if so, did you drink it?"

"Yes, yes, I did. I found it quite thoughtful that we would be offered refreshment. I have not previously experienced being offered tea, much less tea being brought to the passengers, and therefore I thought it was a service provided specifically by this company. Why are you asking about being served tea? Is that not a standard course of fare on this route?"

"I'm not saying that, but merely gathering information to piece together the events before the train arrived at the depot." With that, Drew felt enough had been said. She screwed the top onto the pen and placed it and the notebook back into her satchel. "I won't keep you any longer, Mr. Bennett. Thank you for your time, and for feeding someone who had not come for a social visit."

"I understand that you cannot say more, Miss Davies. You have given me much to think about. I will try again to remember anything else I can and let you know if I do have further recollections."

Drew rose from her chair as did the gentleman, and together they walked to his front door. She held out her hand. "Thank you again for being so generous with your time, and your food! I must say that I hope we have the opportunity, under different circumstances, to talk about your gardens, and I would enjoy knowing more about your writing. Reading and gardening are my greatest pleasures, and I have never met an author before."

"Well, since we are neighbors, I very much look forward to having tea again as well, under less-concerning circumstances. Please don't feel you are disturbing me. If you need to come ask more questions, I am available. I want to help in the investigation however I can."

Drew walked down his front steps, gathered her bicycle and her thoughts, and rode back toward Swansea and the depot to make more notes. While the investigation was much on her mind, the time spent with Mr. Bennett was very enjoyable, and she definitely looked forward to their meeting again.

In the world of mayhem and murder, she reminded herself that he, too, was a suspect. Everyone was a suspect who had been a passenger on that train, and despite appearances and reputations, and until cleared of any involvement in Eireann's death, she needed to maintain an unbiased perspective and professional distance from them all.

CHAPTER 16

A LIFE'S TALE – SATURDAY, MARCH 29

D rew rang the vicarage early to let Liam know that she would be over to work in the gardens, removing any weeds that had decided to pop up.

"Officer Claerk rang a bit ago," said Liam. "They'd like Aunt Theda and me to come to the station this morning. They have some additional questions and would like us to go over our memories of the day again."

"That's fine," said Drew. "I'll be busy in the garden, and we can visit when you return."

She finished in the gardens just before one and let herself into the vicarage to prepare the lunch she had brought for them. Rudy stayed close by her side, hoping for a morsel of the food she placed on the table.

Drew heard the door latch announcing their return just as she finished arranging the table, anticipating they were in need of tea and nourishment. She heard them in mid-conversation as they walked into the cottage.

". . . and why must they ask the same questions over and over? My memory of what occurred has not changed. It is just so upsetting to relive it over and again." Theda heaved a sigh as she turned into the parlor and deposited her handbag and Eireann's yellow coat, which she had taken to wearing, onto the sofa.

"I'm sure Chief Inspector Lewis is hoping you might remember something else— something that may have been overlooked, however small, that might help." Liam tossed his hat onto the sofa and walked with his aunt into the kitchen.

"Lunch! You prepared us lunch, Drew. Whatever you have smells wonderful. How thoughtful of you. I didn't realize it was so late and that I was so hungry." Theda tugged down the front of her dress and turned back to Liam. "But oh my, rehashing the horrible event is completely exhausting. Every time I have to retell what happened I live the pain all over again. I am so grateful that you were with me, dear."

"Of course, Auntie. I would never allow them to question you alone. And Drew, yes, thank you so much for bringing lunch. A most pleasant surprise."

Liam pulled out a chair for his aunt and then sat as Drew poured tea. Rudy seemed to sense the sadness in the house as he circled twice and laid down quietly beside Liam.

"Besides asking you questions, did they answer any of yours? I hope it is alright if I ask."

"Yes, of course. You can ask anything," said Liam. "But *they* did all the asking and very little of the telling. Each time we inquired as to what information they had, they stalled and said it was all under investigation or they still had others to question. You would think *we* were under scrutiny. It was very frustrating."

"I know it's horribly frustrating and painful, but everyone that rode that train *is* a suspect. All you can do is wait and hope they find clues and information leading to the murderer. While I know that is not comforting in any way, I hope lunch will help provide a calm in the day."

Drew took her seat and proceeded to pass a platter of fresh pasta in a dried tomato and mushroom sauce. "Please, help yourselves. You need to eat. I apologize that there isn't bread. We had no flour left this week for baking."

Theda took a large portion and immediately began twirling the pasta onto her fork. "This is delicious, Drew," she managed to say, still savoring her first bite. "Will you be making such lunches often for Liam?"

"No, Auntie. Drew is not required to cook for me. She is hired to clean the vicarage and help keep the gardens tended. No cooking involved."

"He won't need to worry about meals, Miss O'Neill," Drew added, "as the women of the church auxiliary will be bombarding him with casseroles every week."

"Actually, Drew, I told them that, while I much appreciated their offers of meals, I prefer to do my own cooking. That I find it a source of creativity and relaxation."

"Oh, Liam, what foolishness. I do not believe you have ever cooked a meal in your life. Whyever would you tell those kind ladies such nonsense?"

"You well know, Auntie, I have suffered the kindnesses of well-intentioned church auxiliary women at each of my previous postings and soon realized they were not interested in feeding me as much as they were interested in feeding their curiosity. Somehow, they seemed to think entrance into the vicarage granted them permission to ask any number of questions as to my personal life that had nothing to do with the delivery of an overcooked and bland meal."

Drew choked with laughter as she tried to take a swallow of tea and soon all three of them were laughing. It was a much-needed moment of lightheartedness in an otherwise sad and worrisome week.

As though thinking her thoughts aloud, Theda said, "I keep seeing Eireann's body looking so calm and peaceful as she laid in the hospital. So unlike her usual vibrant and busy self. I worried constantly every time she left on what she called an 'errand.' Sometimes one of her so-called errands took her away for days at a time, and never knowing where she went or what she was doing terrified me. I was not with her so how could I protect her, and now, sitting right there beside her on the train, I could not protect her either. They finally found her."

"If you don't mind my asking, what do you mean 'they finally found her?'" asked Drew.

Theda, teary-eyed once again, laid her fork across her empty plate and looked out the window, wiping her damp eyes.

After some moments, Liam laid his hand on his aunt's and said, "Auntie

Theda, why don't you start at the beginning and tell us. I know you and Eireann kept many secrets over all these years, but now it's time to let those go. And we are good listeners."

Theda nodded and turned again to gaze out the window into her past. "Yes, it is time. And how much time do you both have to listen to a rather long story?"

Drew looked at Liam, who nodded and answered for them both. "We have all the time that is needed."

Drew brewed more tea, and as the cups were refilled, she noticed a light drizzle of rain covering the windows, watering the gardens. The room felt cozy, and she felt she was exactly where she needed and wanted to be as Theda began her story.

"Soon after I finished my schooling, I began working in a drapery factory in Belfast. The building included a large warehouse always full of fabric bolts, cutting tables, and sewing machines, with the sales counters set up near the front entrance. The owners did a thriving business.

"That was 1917, and I was eighteen and eager to begin working full-time. My da secured the job for me; he knew the owners and knew that I enjoyed working with fabrics. I was in my teens when I began making all my own clothes and was especially keen on hat design. My employers, the Banningtons, were kind and taught me much about running a business, including the buying of fabrics.

"I continued living at home and worked on my millinery designs in the evenings. My parents encouraged me to show several of the hats I created to my employers in hopes they would allow me to sell them. Not having much confidence, I was surprised when they offered me a small space in the front sales area of the store to display my creations.

"The hats began to sell well, and soon I could not make them fast enough for all the ladies wanting to buy. The Banningtons were making a percentage from each sale and of course were delighted to have these customers in their store, as well as the extra money.

"One day, after staying up late most nights for many months, designing and crafting my creations, I gathered my tired wits about me and spoke to my supervisor. I told him I was not getting any sleep, that between working the sales counter at the drapery during the day and making hats all night, I was done in. I handed him my sales numbers for the last three months and the drapers' percentage of those sales. I told him if I focused my time on designing, making, and selling hats during the day, I felt I could double my sales and therefore double their percentage.

"Da had helped me put together a sales plan that I showed to my boss, including projected sales numbers that would allow me to rent a small space from them. He said he would take it up with Mr. Bannington and his wife and let me know.

"I heard nothing for a week and assumed nothing would come of my proposal. I was surprised when, after ten days went by, Mr. and Mrs. Bannington came to me and asked me to follow them.

"We walked outside the building, then through a door facing the front into a good-sized room. They explained that this had once been used for storage but had been empty for so long they often forgot it existed. But Mrs. Bannington did recall the room when told about my plan. As I said, they were very kind and supportive. We spoke for at least an hour about how the space could work as a millinery shop.

"The door was not far from the main entrance to the drapery and could become the entrance where my customers would come and go. Mrs. Bannington felt the room could be divided into front and back rooms—the front for sales and a showroom and the back as a workroom and storage, where long shelves already lined the walls. They then took me up steep stairs on the back wall to an apartment with four small rooms: a kitchen and sitting room, a bathroom, and a small bedroom.

"At one time, the wife's mam lived there, and after she passed, various family members stayed in the apartment when they visited. They had all passed on and the Banningtons never had children who might have had use for the apartment. They told me if I ever wanted to, I could rent the apartment in addition to the shop space below.

"It was more than I could have dreamed of, and I was overwhelmed with gratitude. I went home that day, still in a daze, and told my parents. What they had not told me was the owners had come to them first and asked what they thought of the idea, and my mam and da had given their wholehearted support. That night, Da and I drew up sketches for the shop and workspace, and the next weekend he and my uncle cleared the space, built a countertop with display shelves below and somewhere found a tired old cash register that still worked.

"Mam and I cleaned all the windows, scrubbed the concrete floors, and planned to paint the walls, when we were able to find paint, that is. And we made curtains for the one window on the outside wall of the room from one of Mam's table coverings. The Banningtons gave me a round table and three chairs for the back room, as well as a large piece of lovely drapery fabric to create a divider between the front and back areas. While Mam and I were at it, we thoroughly cleaned the upper apartment. I already had dreams of living up there on my own."

Theda stopped speaking, took several deep breaths, and asked, "May I please have a glass of water, Drew? Talking is a dry business. I do hope I'm not boring you. I haven't thought about those early times in over thirty years."

"I have never heard this story, Auntie, and it certainly isn't boring. I'm waiting for the part where Eireann and I make our entrance."

"Well, brace yourselves, as the story becomes more interesting from here." Theda drank the water down and went on sharing her memories.

"I opened my millinery shop in 1919 to great fanfare from friends and family, including the Banningtons. They told me I had become like family to them, and they did indeed seem to be as excited as I was.

"After two years in my small shop, my business income allowed me to rent the apartment above, and I moved into that glorious space. I was independent, had a thriving business, and good friends. I felt I had conquered the world.

"I was so busy designing and selling that I often neglected the management of the accounts. The backroom was disorganized, and I never seemed to have time to do everything needed to run a well-managed business. I knew I could not go on like that but was too busy to look for a person to help. I was again working long hours and was always tired.

"One day in the spring of 1921, the door to my shop flew open and a disheveled young woman burst in. I was standing behind the counter as she quickly approached me, then suddenly stepped past me to duck down behind the counter, whispering breathlessly, 'Please help me. Two nasty men are pursuing me, and I need a place to hide—just for a little while.'

"It was not ten seconds after she uttered those words that, indeed, two brutish-looking men entered my shop, asking if I had seen a young woman of such-and-such a height and coloring. Truth be told, I hadn't even had time to take measure of the young woman crouching on the floor beside me.

"I was never one to be flustered in the moment, and I certainly knew those men were not there to ask the girl to tea. I casually looked up from attempting to place a pheasant feather on a hat and told them I had seen no such person, and they might check next door, in the drapery. They looked at me for a moment and then quickly turned and literally ran out of my door. I could see them looking right and left, literally not knowing where to turn.

"Just stay exactly where you are," I quietly told the woman on the floor, "until I am sure they have gone." When I saw them enter the drapery, and felt it safe, I had her crawl into the back room and then follow me up to the apartment. I gave her a glass of water, a flannel, and soap and told her she could freshen up. I would be back when I saw their automobile had gone. The men did not leave for another thirty minutes, time enough for me to form many questions for the mysterious young woman.

"After they finally drove away, I locked my front door, turned the sign to 'CLOSED', and proceeded upstairs, where I found the woman much cleaner and as put together as her torn garments allowed—consisting of a pair of ripped trousers, a man's shirt, and a pair of well-worn boots, which she had taken off and set beside the small kitchen table.

"'I put the kettle on for tea,' she said. 'I can make us a lovely cuppa in no time atall.'

"'Or you could leave now if you like, no questions asked.'

"'I'd rather sit and have tea, if that is alright with you.'

"I do not know why I was interested in what she might have to say, but I did know my heart went out to this person and thought she might need the time to settle herself before she set out once more. I was surprised that, after her initial cry for help when she entered the shop, she now seemed very composed and almost jovial.

"She had obviously looked about and found the teapot, tea, and cups and had not hesitated to set them on the table. I sat as she warmed the pot, then poured the tea to steep, and sat down in the other chair. She ran her hands through very short hair that looked as though she had cut it herself, and quickly at that. She appeared desperately bold, saying, 'Tea is just what we both need after that scare, wouldn't you agree?' She paused and took several long drinks, her eyes darting about, sizing me up but never stopping on my face.

"'And I haven't eaten since I can remember. Being on the run is always chancy, as you never know where you'll end up or with whom. I am very pleased I ended up here, and am greatly in your debt,' she said, refilling our cups.

"'And you have done this before? Been on the run, I mean?' I asked incredulously.

"'Not often, and not by choice, but sometimes circumstances in the moment dictate our course of action. Wouldn't you agree?' She said this with a bright smile that I would come to know so well.

"Not able to help myself, I smiled too, shook my head, and got up to make us something to eat. I was, by now, deeply intrigued and wanted to know more about this unusual woman who literally sprang into my very predictable life.

"I laid plates on the table along with bread, cheese, and slices of apple, and sat again, saying, 'As way of introduction, I am Theda O'Neill, and this is my apartment and my millinery shop below. I was born and raised here in Belfast and no doubt will spend all my remaining days here. Probably, literally, here in this space. And you, what of you?'

"'I am Eireann Swan. I'm not from around here but farther to the south.

Some of my time I spend with my family on their farm, keeping the accounts and milking goats and cows. But I haven't been there for a spell and don't think I'll be returning any time soon, seeing as those same men that came into your shop might come looking for me there. Or someone they think is me. Might we have more tea and maybe some more of that delicious cheese and bread? I'll be happy to pay you back for your generosity.'

"I put the kettle back on, prepared more food, and asked, 'Why are you running? Are you in danger? Your family must be worried sick about you.'

"'Nah, my da and mam stopped worrying for me long ago. They know not to be too concerned. I always take care of myself.'

"I did not ask any more questions, did not have the time, as customers who had appointments were knocking on the front door. An hour had passed, and I needed to open the shop again. All afternoon, customers came and went, and there was no time to think about the curious young woman upstairs.

"Imagine my surprise, several hours later, when I entered the back room to find Eireann there and that the entire room had quietly been put into neat order. One side of the worktable had been randomly piled with fabric, feathers, pins, and the other side was strewn with papers—receipts and bills, letters, and such. She had organized it all and straightened the shelves lining the back wall. The floor had been swept clean of bits of felt and thread, and a few pieces had found rest in her hair.

"She put her hands on her slim hips, gave me that huge smile, and said, 'I can see you need some help with all this. I can do anything but make fine hats.'

"I stood amazed, more at the wonder of her than what she had accomplished. And that smile caught at my heart again as I told her yes. If she was looking for a job and could really do accounting and stock ordering, as well as organizing and keeping things generally in order, I would give her a job. Her smile seemed to grow even wider, and I found myself asking if she had any place to stay. She said not to worry, she would find something and could she start tomorrow.

"Again, I do not know what came over me, but I found myself telling her she could sleep on the sofa upstairs until she found something suitable.

"She gave me a tight hug, saying, 'I'll take you up on your grand offer, Theda. A place to work and a place to sleep. Doesn't get much better than that. Oh, and you don't have to pay me, as I'll work for my board.'

"And with those words, I found myself with a roommate and an employee. The first months, we learned how to work together and live together. She gave me warning early on that from time to time she would need to leave for a few days, maybe a week, and would then return. She did just that. She would come and go every few weeks, or maybe once a month, and then return, and our lives went back to what would become our normal routine. We were both happy with the arrangement, but I missed her terribly when she was away.

"That fall, my younger brother and his wife, Liam's parents, were killed in an accident. Your family lived close by, dear Liam, and I saw you very often from the time you were born; we were all so very close. After your parents passed, you came to live with us. We soon realized the small apartment was no place to raise an active boy, so we moved into your family home, which your parents left to me until you were of age. As I said, your da and I were close, your mam as well, as we were the only family each had. Our own parents, including your mam's, died when we were all in our twenties.

"When you came to live with us after we moved into the house, it was a challenging time of adjustment for all of us. You were the sweetest of children, and your sadness broke our hearts. After a couple months of finding our way, we settled in and became a family. We were content and life went on.

"After your parents passed and we were in the house for a month or so, Eireann told me we had to have a serious talk. I thought perhaps she wanted to leave, that maybe she did not want a child about. But I never dreamed I'd hear what she had to say.

"Eireann was an undercover intelligence volunteer for the Irish Republican Army. All her comings and goings over the years that we had been together were because of her clandestine work. It could be dangerous for anyone associated with her as well as for herself. She said she should have told me sooner, but she was afraid of losing me. And now that we were to care for a child, it was time she

literally have nowhere else to while away the time in this miniscule village, I end up bringing them here and spending hours at your quaint library. Therefore, is it really too much to ask that I be provided a cup of tea?" The woman's face was turning red and her hands flew about as her agitation increased.

Neither Lillian nor Charlotte blinked at the woman's outrage.

"Mrs. Archer, while it would indeed be nice to offer tea, we are not permitted to do so. Perhaps I might suggest you and your children step out for tea at one of our lovely tea rooms close by," said Lillian, always calm and serene and now with just a hint of color rising to her cheeks.

Drew knew the librarian was attempting to maintain a professional demeanor as she endeavored, without much success, to quell Eva's temper tantrum.

Apparently forgetting her very proper English accent, Eva, in a very loud and pronounced Irish brogue, responded, "No! It would *not* be a good time. The children are quiet right now, but if I even suggest leaving, they will revolt. And if I do not get my afternoon tea, I will be on the verge of revolt myself!"

Drew stepped forward, interjecting. "Excuse me, Mrs. Archer. I'm Drew Davies, you may remember that we spoke earlier in the week when we met on the beach? I just arrived at the library and plan to spend an hour browsing for books. I would be more than happy to keep an eye on your children while you step out for tea. Would that be helpful?"

Eva stood up straight, her tall frame having been bent halfway over the counter during her tirade. She turned to Drew, smoothed her gray wool dress down the front of her as she struggled to reassemble the pieces of herself, and reverted to her polished English accent. "Well, good afternoon, Miss Davies. This woman and I—"

"Her name is Lillian Powell, and she is our very courteous and capable head librarian."

"So you say, Miss Davies. And you say as well that you are willing to mind my dear children for the next hour?"

"It would be no bother, Mrs. Archer. Would you like to introduce me to them and then you can be on your way?"

"My children are perfectly capable of introducing themselves, so I will be off. Thank you, Miss Davies." Eva grabbed her coat and handbag from atop the counter and fled for the door as if for her life.

Drew looked at Lillian and Charlotte, and the three attempted to suppress their astonishment as well as their muted laughter at the desperate behavior of the woman.

"Thank you for saving me, Drew," said Lillian, sotto voce. That woman has been pestering Charlotte and myself each and every day, insisting on being served tea since the first time she darkened the library's door. I do believe we will both need something a little stronger in our tea than mere milk this afternoon, would you not agree, dear Charlotte?

"Lillian, you rapscallion," said Drew. "I distinctly heard you tell Mrs. Archer there was to be no tea."

"Not to patrons in the main library with all the precious books, but certainly to those of us who work here behind our desk and," she added looking to Drew with a smile, "to those that help us contain rowdy patrons. And since you are taking care of her children, that entitles you to an extra cup as well." Charlotte, Lillian's partner in all things, grinned in complicity as she rose to head to the back room where the kettle and cups were kept.

"I'll go introduce myself to her children while the water boils and return shortly." Drew found the young boy and older girl in the children's section around the corner from the front desk. The boy was sprawled on the floor lying on his stomach, knees bent, his legs slowly wiggling back and forth in the air. He seemed completely absorbed in whatever he was reading. The girl was on the sofa under the window, equally at ease and equally focused on her book of choice. Drew stood and watched them for a little while, hating to disturb their reveries.

She sat down on the floor in front of the boy, her back against the sofa where the girl sat, and said, "Hello, children. My name is Drew, and I told your mother, who I've recently met, that she could go enjoy a cup of tea, and I would visit with the two of you until she returned."

With raised eyebrows, both children looked up at Drew, then at each other, and immediately dove back into their readings, as if Drew's voice had been something they thought they might have heard and decided they had not.

Sitting patiently waiting for a response and getting none, Drew asked, "And what are your names? How old might you be?"

The children looked at Drew again, then at one another, and some type of unspoken agreement must have passed between them, for the decision to answer this stranger's questions was made.

"My name is Penny," said the girl, "and I am eleven but will soon be twelve."

"I'm Braden, and I am nine but not almost ten."

Penny continued looking at Drew while her brother spoke again. "We saw you at the beach the other day, talking with Mammy. Are you friends?"

"You are right. I was there talking with her, but that was the first time we met. Do you enjoy the beach here in Mumbles?"

"It's alright," said Braden, "but awfully cold. Do you know how much longer we'll be at the library today? We like it here."

"Your mother said she will be back in one hour."

Again, the two locked eyes and shook their heads as the girl replied, "You may find yourself with us for more than an hour. Perhaps two, at least. Mam never returns when she intends to. We are fine by ourselves if you would rather leave. We fend for ourselves most of the time and are quite used to it." The girl gave a half-convincing smile and a very convincing sigh of sad resignation.

"The library is truly my favorite place in Mumbles," said Drew. "I am here often borrowing new books, returning others, or just finding a cozy spot to read, as you are doing. So, if you don't mind, I will browse the shelves until your mother returns."

Penny and Braden nodded and went back to their reading. They certainly did not seem the uncontrollable and rowdy children their mother painted them to be. Perhaps they were tired or didn't feel well. Perhaps they were hungry.

Shortly after his mother departed, Braden had fallen asleep on the floor, and Drew asked Lillian for something to cover him with.

Penny looked up as Drew approached with a shawl and smiled; the girl had a lovely smile. She reached for the covering and laid it gently across her brother.

Mrs. Archer returned to her children just as the library was closing, almost two hours after she had gone in search of a proper tea. "Thank you, Miss Davies," said Eva, observing her sleeping son beginning to rouse at the sound of his mother's voice. "I appreciate your taking the time to mind my offspring. I do hope they behaved themselves. Gather up your belongings, children, we need to meet your father for dinner. Hurry along now."

Eva turned and headed for the entrance before Braden had completely woken and gotten to his feet. Yawning, he picked up two books, took his sister's ready hand, and together they followed their mother out the door.

"Thank you for your kindness, Miss Davies. Maybe we will see you here again," said Penny, smiling over her shoulder.

The three women stood silent, watching despairingly as the family left the library.

"We kept the kettle simmering, Drew. Now come and have your tea."

CHAPTER 18

THE TEACUP, TUESDAY, APRIL 1

Before they sat for their tea, Charlotte turned the lock on the library door, officially closing the building for the day. She took Drew by the arm and led them into the small room behind the front counter. Lillian had set a plate of butter biscuits and three mismatched china cups and saucers on the round wooden table.

As Drew and Charlotte sat down, one of the teacups caught Drew's eye, and she picked it up and turned it over. "Has this collection of cups always been here, Lillian?"

"Oh, I have picked them up at shops as they have caught my eye over the years. Why do you ask?"

"The cup I'm holding is identical to the two I found in the passenger coach where Miss Swan was killed."

Charlotte looked closely at the cup in Drew's hand. "That one I brought with me from London when I moved here last year. I thought I might add a couple of my own to the library's collection. We already have more than we need at the house." Lillian had offered Charlotte a room to rent in her home until she found her own place after moving to Mumbles following her father's death. The women quickly bonded, became companions, and now shared Lillian's home as their own.

Drew nodded and continued examining the cup. "The bottom is marked with the same symbol and writing as the ones on the train. Those were somewhat hard to make out, but this one is easily deciphered: 'Ireland', with a picture of a lion with a crown on its head."

"May I?" said Charlotte, holding out her hand. "The symbols on the bottom of fine porcelain plates and cups or vases and pottery are called maker's marks or backstamps. The 'Ireland' designation indicates where the piece was made, the country of origin. The color of the stamp, in this case green, denotes the time in which that particular piece of china was crafted. The picture of the lion wearing the crown is the company's personal maker's mark."

"I've never noticed markings on the bottom of anything before, Charlotte. You are always such a wealth of information. And because of that," said Drew, as a thought entered her mind, "would you be willing to do some sleuthing on the side for me?"

"Absolutely! That sounds as though it could be quite interesting. What is it you need?"

"Because this cup is identical to the ones I found, it may be important to find out what company made them, where and when it was made, and if that company is still in existence."

Lillian chimed in at this point. "Actually, we have a book here that lists all the major manufacturers of fine china in Europe. I'll just pop up and find it. Be right back."

"And Charlotte, I need more information on three people. One of whom is your library acquaintance, Eva Archer. She claims to be a renowned stage actress, and I have a short article about a London production she was in some years ago. I'd like to know where she was born and more about her life and career.

"And her husband, Rex Archer. He appears to be a wealthy man. She says he is an only child who inherited quite a bit of money from his father. According to her, he has a business in Belfast. He is also a self-proclaimed plein-air painter and told me that he brought his family to Wales so he could 'paint the light.' Could you find out what you can about him as well?"

Charlotte had secured a pencil and paper and began taking notes, attempting to keep up with Drew's requests. "Oh, indeed this will be interesting! I may visit the university library in London for a day of research. It will be good to be on the campus again, and as a retired professor, I have lifetime access to the library. I may even go tomorrow."

"Here we are," said Lillian, returning with a rather large book and setting it down on the table. She laid it open and indicated a list of what Drew assumed were china factories. "The green color of the maker's mark on this cup indicates it was produced in the 1920s. The symbol of the lion is one of a very old and prestigious company in Belfast, Gallagher and Sons, Ltd."

"Thank you, Lillian. How lucky to have all that information right here at our fingertips."

Lillian smiled. "Yes, many don't realize that libraries hold all the information amassed throughout time. You just need to know where to look for it."

"I have one more person I would like information on: a Mr. William Bennett. He, too, arrived on the train with Miss Swan and Miss O'Neill and shared the same passenger carriage. I have spoken with him at some length, and he says he just moved to Mumbles from Belfast, that he is a writer seeking a quieter place to live and work. He has purchased an older cottage close to my family's. He is a gentleman in his fifties and has a daughter named Eileen Bennett, whom he says is a physician. She will be seeking a position in the area, perhaps in Swansea. At any rate, I would like to know more about Mr. Bennett and anything regarding his daughter."

Lillian raised her eyebrows. "Mr. William Bennett is indeed a highly acclaimed writer of literary fiction. I'm sure you know of him as well, Charlotte."

"Of course," replied Charlotte. "There must be several books authored by him right here in the library. Would that be correct?" she said, turning to Lillian.

Lillian nodded and disappeared through the door, apparently to seek out novels by Mr. Bennett.

"You two are amazing. I don't know what to say except thank you for your help."

"Well," said Charlotte, "do not thank us until we have gathered all the information you requested. Hopefully it proves helpful. Then you can thank us all you wish."

Lillian reappeared, this time with two books by William Bennett. "I've read these and there are two more on the shelf. I think you would enjoy Mr. Bennett's writing, Drew. Something other than your mysteries perhaps," she said with a grin. "I'll check them out for you. We plan to invite him to do a reading here, once he settles in, of course."

Drew held up the teacup. "And may I hold onto this please?"

Both women nodded.

The three of them began gathering up the remains of the tea and made quick work of washing up. Drew put the books and teacup into her satchel, and they all headed home for the night.

As Drew pedaled down the lane, she thought how very fortunate she was to have such friends: kind, humorous, and very well-informed. Perfect to have around when a murder needed solving.

EASTER SUNDAY – APRIL 6, 1947

Easter morning dawned overcast and threatening as Theda waited anxiously for Drew, Howard, and Naomi just inside the church vestibule. When they arrived, Drew took her arm, and they followed her grandparents into the wide expanse of the church.

Theda was dressed in a lovely navy-blue dress with a matching hat. Nonna wore a hat as well, but not being one for hats, Drew conveniently forgot hers at home. Drew thought Granda very handsome in his good summer suit. He had removed his hat before asking for four worship programs from the congregant who welcomed each person as they entered.

As they moved down the center aisle to a pew on the right side toward the middle front, Granda motioned for the women to go ahead to their seats and he followed. The pews were filling quickly, and Drew expected the church to be full on this Easter Sunday. The faithful and the curious would come to watch the new vicar deliver his first sermon, he a somewhat novice vicar whose family member had been murdered only two weeks before.

The murder remained unsolved, and the populace were perhaps hoping for great theatre as well as expecting a passable sermon. Drew prayed that Liam was up to the task, even when she knew his heart was aching.

As organ music began with a rousing Easter anthem, the people rose from their seats and the choir proceeded down the aisle to take their places on the benches behind the alter. Liam followed, resplendent in his clerical vestments, a black cassock under a white surplice, his hands held still in front of him as he walked to the front of the church.

He stepped up into the pulpit, raised his arms toward the congregation, and said, "Alleluia! Christ is risen!" The congregation responded as one, saying, "He is risen indeed."

As everyone sat and the church became silent, all eyes watched Liam glance upward and pause before looking directly at those he came to address. "On this first Sunday as your new vicar, I extend to you sincere Easter greetings. And although my heart is heavy, my spirit is joyful to be here with you all. As most of you know, I recently lost a beloved family member, Eireann Swan, in the most grievous of circumstances. My aunt, Theda O'Neill, and I have been making difficult arrangements following her death. This was not how I expected the first few weeks in a new parish to proceed as I prepared to deliver an Easter message of resurrection and joy.

"But life often delivers us unexpected turns in the road. Around some we find joy, and around others we find sorrow. Occasionally, we find both around the same bend, as I have since arriving in this beautiful country.

"Yesterday morning, I went fishing on a placid tree-lined lake, a small lake not far from here. I dug up worms from the garden's soil at the vicarage, took up my pole, whistled to my dog, Rudy, and we were off. After two hours of patience and fortitude, not a single fish had come to my hook.

"But what I did catch was the ear of our Creator. He was also patient and showed great fortitude as I poured out my heart. I cried, complained, demanded, pleaded, and begged for an answer to the one question that plagues humans: Why? Why had Eireann died, and why, when I was a young child, did my own parents die? Why do unbearable things happen to us and to those we love? Why, oh Lord?

"About that time, I believe God turned and whispered to St. Michael, 'Doesn't he sound just like Job?' But God's ear is always tuned to us. Whether we are rejoicing or in the depths of despair, He tells us again and again He is there and always listening, always caring for us. First Peter 5:7 tells us to 'cast all your anxiety on Him because He cares for you.'

"Sometimes as believers, if we allow ourselves to feel the depth of our pain or acknowledge the burdens of life, we feel ashamed or even guilty. We think if we were more faithful, we would never feel as sad as we sometimes do, never be as angry as we are, never feel life is unjust or unfair. But being created in the image of God, and knowing the struggles Christ went through, we are in good company. Jesus never pretended his life was easy. He suffered a life of injustice.

"Our Creator knows we have a whole host of emotions that are sometimes glorious and sometimes dreadful. The glorious moments need to be celebrated in gratitude. The difficult times need to be acknowledged and shared honestly with the Lord and with those that love us. Those that can surround us in love and support us.

"So yesterday, on that body of water, I poured out my heart and the Lord listened. He was happy to do so, and I was blessed. He does not judge our pain. He sees our pain and hears our pleas.

"And we have the answer to all our 'whys.' Because life is hard. The good news, the great news is that today is Easter Sunday, and our Lord can ease our hearts, and even in the midst of pain, there can be joy.

"I came off that lake yesterday feeling a peace I had not felt in a great while. We do not know all or sometimes any of the answers to the 'whys' of life, but we know God is in His heaven, and we can rest in that place of peace now and forever.

"Alleluia, Christ is risen."

The congregation responded in kind and the choir stood and sang *"Christ the Lord is Risen Today."* On the last verse, Liam left the pulpit and walked down the aisle, followed by the choir.

Remaining in the pew as others moved toward the refreshments waiting in the common room, Drew turned to Theda. "He was wonderful, wasn't he? Now, if you'd rather go back to the vicarage than stay, I am happy to accompany you."

"I do, thank you, but I will see Liam through his first Sunday. One that I know is very difficult. I also know he is glad you are here, dear, as am I."

Many of those attending the service had gone directly home to prepare their Easter dinners, including her grandparents. Still, the common room was full of those staying to have a word with their new vicar. Everyone speaking to Liam seemed genuinely pleased and most likely relieved that the service had gone well. Drew heard them congratulate him on a fine first sermon, and offer him wishes for a happy Easter and many expressions of sympathy.

Theda wiped her eyes and spoke softly to Drew. "Everyone seems quite pleased with Liam's first service. I know I am certainly proud of him. How fortunate they are to have such a fine young vicar."

"Ie, they are, Miss O'Neill. You and Eireann raised a fine man. You should be proud of yourself as well."

Theda gave Drew's arm a squeeze as she stepped toward the nicely decorated table adorned with cookies of every variety, all made, Drew was sure, by the Women's Auxiliary. Many rations of sugar and flour had been reserved for this day.

Drew remained where she stood, watching as Theda, a plate of cookies in one hand and a cup of tea in the other, made her way to stand beside her beloved nephew. Liam looked up, searching for Drew, and when he found her smiled his glorious smile and nodded his head. She did the same in return, hoping she would see them both again in the next few days.

Knowing Granda and Nonna were waiting for her, Drew set about for home. The three of them, along with some friends, were going to Serena's home for dinner. She hoped Liam and Theda would be able to rest this afternoon. She knew they would have an abundance of food brought to them by the caring women of the church.

Drew walked slowly, thinking how poised Liam was with all the attention and how gracious were his responses to the congregants. He exuded an aura of compassion tinged with a trace of sadness that she thought was a part of his soul. She found herself wanting to come alongside him, protecting him from ever having his heart broken again.

CHAPTER 20

SLEUTHING LIBRARIANS – WEDNESDAY, APRIL 9

The next Wednesday found Drew pedaling as quickly as she could to get home from the depot and change her clothes. Charlotte and Lillian were waiting for her. A light rain was starting, so she donned her wellies and mackintosh before heading out the door for a brisk walk to the library.

Charlotte had rung yesterday asking if she could come over after work. They had much to tell her regarding the Archers, and also William Bennett. As the rain began in earnest and her anticipation rose, Drew nearly ran to the library.

She blew through the front doors along with the wind and rain, wiped her boots on the rug just inside the door, and proceeded toward her friends. They were both standing in anticipation behind the front counter, their auras bright and shining, and Drew was sure hers, although slightly wet, was as well.

As Drew approached them, Lillian said in a whisper, "There are several people still here. Charlotte can check them out, and I will shelve the remaining books, close for the evening, and then we can talk. We've found out a great deal!"

Drew nodded and moved off to browse the shelves. She could feel her excitement and was curious what information Charlotte could have acquired in London. So many possibilities. She had to smile at her friends' air of mystery.

She was so appreciative of their help, these two intelligent women who had become such dear friends.

She found another of William Bennett's books, and because she had enjoyed his first two novels, she pulled the third from the shelf and went to a seat by the window to have a look. Waiting was never a strong suit of Drew's, and she found the time moving so slowly she felt she might explode.

Thirty more minutes passed before the last of the patrons checked out their books and left. Lillian locked the library doors as Charlotte moved two chairs up beside Drew's.

"Alright, you two, I am bursting with curiosity. What have you found?"

"You begin, Charlotte. Tell her about Eva, her family, and Rex, and then I'll share what I found out about Bennett."

Charlotte put on her reading glasses, cleared her throat, crossed her legs at her ankles, and opened a journal to begin. "Well, it took some digging at the library in London, but I eventually found numerous newspaper articles and references in various tomes regarding a Mr. Terence Gallagher, Eva Archer's father. For what it's worth, Terence is an ancient Celtic name, also related to the Old Norse "Thórr," who was the god of thunder, and it is a common name among many Irish families, including the Gallaghers." Charlotte had a penchant for knowing a trove of arcane facts and loved to present them whether it was timely or not.

"Mr. Gallagher was a fourth-generation businessman and a very prominent figure in the Belfast community. His large and very prosperous company, Gallagher and Son, Ltd., produced the very finest of Irish porcelain and bone china dinnerware, including the teacups you found in the carriage. The mark on the bottom of the teacup confirms it was manufactured by Mr. Gallagher's company.

"There were many articles regarding his involvement with various organizations in Belfast. He was also known as a strong Loyalist and supported the continued existence of Ireland within the United Kingdom. He fiercely opposed a free Ireland, independent of Britain.

"However, I could not find any instances where Mr. Gallagher was directly involved in supporting the Loyalist cause. By that, I mean there were no specific articles or reports of him participating in any opposition against the activities of the IRA. However, what I read seemed to infer that he did offer support by way of significant monetary donations. So much that happened during that time, on both sides, was done clandestinely and certainly not reported, for fear of reprisals. It would be hard to determine the extent of Mr. Gallagher's support and involvement."

Charlotte stopped there, removed her glasses, and took a drink of water. "Any questions? If not, I will go on."

Drew was held in rapt attention, quickly making notes in her own journal. "Ie, do go on, Charlotte. This is all fascinating."

"The conflicts from 1920 through 1922 occurred primarily between the Irish Loyalists and the Nationalists. The members of the Irish Republican Army were part of the Nationalist movement that wanted a united Ireland, free and independent from the British. The violence between the Loyalist and the Nationalist factions turned deadly, most of it centered in Belfast. Bombings and explosions were frequent, and many homes and businesses were destroyed, including Mr. Gallagher's. Gallagher, forty-five years old at the time, and his son, Owen, twenty-one, were both killed in a blast that destroyed his factory. The IRA was taking responsibility for many of the Belfast bombings, so . . .

"I found no reference to Mrs. Gallagher, other than in her husband's and son's obituaries. There was nothing regarding Eva, their daughter, until she made the papers as an actress on the stages of London and then again in the social columns, when she married Rex Archer. She was in several theatrical productions in London, but about the time her children would have been born, she abruptly left acting and returned to Ireland. It does not appear that she continued her acting career in Ireland after having her second child. I found nothing more about her once it made the papers that she had returned to Belfast with Rex.

"Rex, as you know, inherited his wealth, and has lived his life traveling and painting. From what I could ascertain, he supports such a lifestyle from family trust fund monies and has also maintained a working interest in the textile company his father owned. I found no references or articles ever mentioning that Archer had any involvement in any IRA activities, including providing monetary support. But of course, as I previously said, those affairs were most always conducted clandestinely. It was, however, well known that his family were staunch Loyalists.

"So that is the extent of what I found. I do hope it is helpful, Drew." Charlotte removed her glasses once again and took several swallows of water.

"I sit here amazed at your information, Charlotte, and yes, it is most helpful. Eva and Rex are both ongoing suspects in Eireann's murder, and Liam's aunt Theda shared with us that Eireann had been an operative for the IRA in Belfast and participated in undercover operations in 1922. The fact that Eva's father and brother were killed in an IRA bombing and Rex was a known Loyalist makes me wonder if it was more than coincidence that they were on that train with Eireann.

"I need a drink of water and a good stretch," said Drew, "and then we can hear what you found, Lillian."

"I'll get the water for us this time," said Charlotte as Lillian put on her reading glasses and opened a small book. Drew paced the floor until Charlotte returned.

Once they were seated again, Lillian began. "While I did not find the wealth of background information on Mr. Bennett that Charlotte amassed regarding the Gallaghers and the Archers, I was able to reach out to several friends in the community of historical librarians, including some in Belfast. Mr. Bennett was, and perhaps still is, a Loyalist, who has always supported Ireland remaining part of the United Kingdom. He wrote a treatise in 1922 strongly condemning the terrorist acts of the Nationalists and the IRA. The County Antrim library, in Belfast, sent me, on loan of course, Mr. Bennett's small bound volume which I thought you might want to read, Drew." Lillian handed Drew the book, which had been lying on the side table next to her. The book was bound in thick, heavy paper and was, by the looks of it, much worn from frequent readings.

"Thank you, Lillian, I will read it through and return it to you in a few days."

Lillian went on, "I found no other mention of any political involvement by Mr. Bennett. I've read all his books and works, and in all of his writings he continually proposes peace. They always support remaining part of Great Britain as the most beneficial way for a turbulent Ireland to become once again a prosperous country free from war.

"One more thing, which may be significant," said Lillian. "The only mention of his family was from an interview the BBC did with him many years ago. He shared that he and his wife had one daughter, Eileen, and that his wife had died tragically in an IRA bombing in 1922. I found no information on Eileen Bennett."

"Thank you, Lillian. That is indeed helpful. While Mr. Bennett proclaims his desire for peace, it doesn't rule out the fact that he may also have been involved in activities in opposition to the IRA. Again, he would have had opportunity on the train to place poison in the tea and, because of his wife's tragic death at the hands of the IRA, would also have motive to kill the person he thought responsible. But why would he leave Ireland and move to another country when he so strongly advocates for his homeland? Does Mr. Bennett frequent our library?"

"Why yes, he comes in at least once a week, always with several books to return and checking more out. He is certainly an avid reader. He chats with us, and we find him to be quite a lovely man. Wouldn't you agree?" said Lillian, turning to Charlotte.

"Oh indeed. He appears to be a gentleman and a scholar, and it is a pleasure to engage him in conversation. He also displays a subtle sense of humor. Which is always a fine attribute in a person. I do believe him to be a man of solid character."

Drew knew Charlotte to be quite a serious woman, and to hear her talk of a sense of humor as being a 'fine attribute' caught Drew off guard and caused her to smile. "I feel the same, however, I did not have occasion to witness his sense of humor. But that is most likely due to the fact that I was questioning him in regard to a murder he may know more about than he let on," she said, raising her eyebrows for emphasis.

The two older women yawned in unison, and Drew realized it was now quite late. They all needed to be off to home.

"Thank you again for shedding so much light on these people and their lives. What excellent researchers you are."

"It was our pleasure. We ask only that you keep us informed regarding your investigation, and let us know if there is any other means by which we can be of assistance," said Lillian.

"Oh my!" exclaimed Charlotte. "I nearly forgot! I found one more article, Drew, which I copied out. In light of the information we gathered, I think you will find it quite interesting." Drew took the folded paper Charlotte handed to her and placed it in her satchel to read when she got home.

With that, they rose as one, picked up their belongings, and headed out into the damp night, Drew's mind working on the possibilities of motive and opportunities to commit murder.

CHAPTER 21

FATHER AND DAUGHTER – THURSDAY, APRIL 10

Drew stepped onto the stone path approaching Mr. Bennett's cottage and was again transported to a place of tranquility. There was an almost magical allure to the gardens, now neatly tended and trimmed. She saw, too, that the window shutters had been replaced and painted a sage green, which was a perfect contrast to the refreshed sandstones of the cottage. The front door was painted a dark brown and the green tendrils of the wisteria that had nearly covered the front entrance had been expertly trimmed to form a welcoming arch above the door. It had been only a week since she was here last, and she wondered at how so much had been accomplished in that short time. Mr. Bennett had indeed been busy making his new cottage a home.

Before knocking, Drew stood at the door and turned to view the gardens. It had rained the night before, and fat drops sat like molten silver glistening on the tops of leaves and fronds, the morning air musky and enticing.

She was startled out of her spell when the door was opened suddenly by a tall, slender woman with dark hair and darker eyes. She did not appear welcoming.

"I've been watching you from the window, wondering why a stranger would take such an interest in my da's gardens. But he said he had been expecting you . . . Miss Davies, I believe he said your name was? Have you finished your inspection? Are you ready to come inside?"

"Oh, good day! Ie, I am here to speak with your father, and I assume you must be Eileen."

"Yes, I suppose I must be. Da said to let you in while he makes himself more presentable than he was when you last questioned him. Have a seat at the kitchen table. I suppose you want tea again as well?"

"No, thank you, I have no need of tea. I will just wait quietly for your father," Drew said, sitting on the same chair she occupied previously, readying her journal and pen. Today, though chilly, found the hearth empty of a fire and no water warming on the plate. And Miss Eileen Bennett was as chilly as the cottage.

"Your father said he was hoping you would be coming for a visit. How long might you be able to stay?"

"Really, Miss Davies, what I do or don't do has no relevance as to why you are here today. I am, however, interested to know why you would possibly need to talk again with my da regarding the death of that woman on the train. Surely you know he had nothing to do with her murder."

Drew maintained the same level of intense eye contact as the curt woman. "Were you also on that train, Miss Bennett?"

As though on cue, William Bennett bustled into the kitchen. "Ah, I hope you two have introduced yourselves. It is nice to see you again, Miss Davies. Eileen, would you be good enough to put the kettle on, and we'll enjoy a cuppa while we chat."

"It's nice to see you again as well, Mr. Bennett. And I must say your front gardens look lovely. As do your shutters and door. You have been very busy since last we spoke."

"I told you then there was much to be done, and I have enjoyed the effort. I found a retired gentleman eager to help with the repairs to the cottage, and he will soon begin working on the roof. As he works on the exterior, I work in the gardens. The beds around back will need much more attention than the ones up front. I am measuring my days between my gardening and my writing. What a perfect balance it is proving to be."

"It's all looking magical." And there, she did it again! Unexpected words flew from her mouth. What was it about being in the presence of this man that caused her to be so unguarded? It was most disconcerting.

Mr. Bennet gave a low-throated chuckle. "Ah, I feel exactly the same, Miss Davies. I am glad we share the sentiment."

The gentleman smiled at Drew and the cottage took on a brightness that warmed the room. She realized it was emanating from his aura, a lovely calm green. Drew looked at his daughter, a scowl about her mouth and a gray swirl surrounding her, so much in contrast to her father. These two were distinct opposites. Drew wondered if the daughter carried the personality traits of her mother or if she was just burdened down by life.

Eileen moved to the table and placed two cups down with hard knocks on the wood surface and a harder look at Drew. No saucers were provided, and neither her father nor Drew made comment to it. The woman turned back, poured hot water over the tea, not bothering to warm the pot, and brought it to the table.

"Thank you for the tea, Miss Bennett, and thank you, Mr. Bennett, for speaking with me again today. I have more information regarding the death of Eireann Swan. She was indeed murdered. The authorities believe she was intentionally poisoned when drinking a cup of tea served as the train was about to pull into the Swansea depot. So far, I don't know if a motive has been determined or any probable suspects identified."

"And what, Miss Davies, does any of this have to do with Da?" Eileen demanded, interrupting Drew.

"As I told him previously, Miss Bennett, as employees of the railway, we are keeping up with the investigation and feel we have an obligation to aid the authorities in any way we can. That includes following up on previous conversations, such as I am having with your father today."

"I am well aware that you are a railway employee, but I fail to understand why you are again needlessly wasting his time."

Rather than responding to the fractious woman, Drew looked at Mr. Bennett and said, "I'm hoping you might, after having had some time to reflect on what happened in the train carriage that day—and seeing as you were the first person to respond to the situation—you might have recalled additional details. Specifically, I would like to ask you to describe the person that walked the aisle offering the passengers tea. Please try to recall any details that come to mind: what were they wearing, their particular physical features, their voice . . . anything at all."

"Since you were last here, I *have* spent time considering the sequence of events that day. While I initially assumed the person dressed in the railway uniform was a man, I do not know if that was actually the case. The only word they said, a question really, was 'Tea?' I do remember the voice gave me no reason to think the individual was not a man.

"They were quite tall and rather rotund. Their hair was covered by a railway cap, and although I assumed both the cap and the uniform were Great Western issue, I really have no idea if that is true. What I did recall later was their eyebrows: they were dark and bushy, and the person's face very ruddy in color, again causing me to assume that it was a man handing me the cup. Is that the person suspected of poisoning the passenger?"

"I have wondered the same," said Drew, "but I don't know if that is what the police suspect."

Eileen rose from the table and huffed away to the rear part of the cottage.

William's eyes followed Eileen for a brief moment before returning his attention to Drew. "Please excuse my daughter. She is quite upset that I have been, in her words, 'dragged into this situation,' even though she realizes that I am still a suspect until the murderer is found.

"She was equally distressed by the young policeman, Constable Claerk, when he came round yesterday. But I find your questions to be more specific, Miss Davies. I do believe you are doing an excellent job for your railway company."

"Thank you, Mr. Bennett, and of course, I understand a daughter wanting to protect her father. I wonder, was Eileen aboard the train that day? You said she wanted to meet with physicians in Swansea, but I did not see her in the depot when everyone gathered in the waiting room."

"We had planned on traveling together; she even purchased a ticket. But at the last minute, she decided to travel on to London, as there was a position she thought might possibly be suitable. She only just arrived here the day before last, after her meetings in Swansea. I am hoping she will be here at least another week or so."

Drew had been making notes in her journal as Mr. Bennett spoke but now paused. The man's eyes were full of concern for his daughter and her future. "I hope she finds a situation that works well for her."

"She told me last night that she doesn't feel the medical practice in London nor the one in Swansea is right for her at this time. I think she may be thinking of returning to Belfast. I was hoping that she might find something to her liking closer to where I have landed, but that doesn't sound like a possibility. We always want our children to find their own way, their own happiness, and we can't expect it to be beside our own."

Drew had suspected his daughter had been listening surreptitiously to their conversation and was even more convinced when she suddenly flew through the room, wrapped in a heavy jumper, and stormed out the door.

"May I ask you, sir, when did your wife, Eileen's mother, pass away?"

Mr. Bennett's eyes immediately became moist and his aura cloudy as he quietly responded to Drew's question. "She was tragically killed in a bombing by IRA radicals during the troubles in '22. I believe Eileen's smoldering anger began the day her mother died and continues to this day."

Drew laid her pen aside and found herself gently placing her hand atop the gentleman's arm. "I am sorry. I lost both my parents and older brother when I was very young. They died under what I still believe to be questionable circumstances. I understand Eileen's lingering grief, as I am sure you do as well. The sadness never really leaves."

Mr. Bennett placed his hand on Drew's. "I am equally sorry for your own loss, my dear. I only wish my daughter could move past the anger and embrace the good that could be her life, as you seem to have done, Miss Davies."

Drew gently removed her hand from under his, nodding in silent agreement, then capped her pen, closed her journal, and placed both into her satchel. She finished the cup of lukewarm tea, pushed her chair back to stand, as did William Bennett, and together they walked to the door.

"By the way, I wanted to let you know that I checked two of your books out of the library—the first two you wrote. I am partway through the second and am very much enjoying your writing. I believe you call your style 'literary fiction.' Since I read mostly mysteries and period novels by women, I find your writing is broadening my literary world."

"Well, I am thinking that is high praise coming from such a young person, and I hope that sometime soon we might find ourselves discussing books and literature rather than murder."

"I look forward to that time as well, Mr. Bennett. Thank you for meeting with me again."

William opened the door for Drew, and she stepped outside to find Eileen standing beside her bicycle.

"I assume you are done with these visits to my da. Because I must insist that you not bother him again. You must be convinced that he knows nothing about the death of that woman. Why on earth would he?"

Drew settled her satchel across her body and pulled up her bike by the handlebars. Before mounting the seat, she turned to Eileen and asked, "Were you aboard the train, Miss Bennett? When Eireann Swan was poisoned?"

"I heard Da tell you that I was not. That I had decided to stay in London. I only arrived here two days ago."

"I know what you told your father, but I don't know it to be the truth. I am truly sorry you lost your mother, Miss Bennett. I hope you might find some peace."

Drew mounted her bicycle and, without a backward glance, made her way home, pondering the stark differences between father and daughter. Perhaps the cottage was filled with malice as well as magic.

CHAPTER 22

AN AWKWARD INTRODUCTION – FRIDAY, APRIL 11

All eyes were on Liam's tall figure and confident stride as he walked through the Swansea station's office door straight to Drew's desk.

"Good day, all, and hello, Drew. I brought you evidence of the surprise I found in the gardens this morning."

"The pussy willows bloomed! How lovely they are, Liam, and how thoughtful of you. This is such a nice surprise." And a surprise it was, as the last person Drew would have expected to visit her at the station was Liam. She had felt her heart leap at the sight of him.

"You are more than welcome. Aunt Theda cut a mass of them, and they look quite nice on the kitchen table."

With a nod of his head, the young man said, "I'll not disrupt you any longer. A good day to each of you."

"Wait! I'd like you to meet some of the people I work with." Drew stood and pointed to each person as she introduced them. "You've met my granda, Howard Davies, the station master and dispatcher, and this is Jonesy, a conductor, and Sam Provens is a railway driver. There are more of us, but they are out and about the station."

"Very nice to meet you all. Again, good day." With a smile and another nod, Liam made his way to the door.

His departure was met with a silence full of curiosity that lingered thoughout the office.

Jonesy was the first to speak. "What man brings the weed of a tree to a young woman he favors? This new vicar seems a bit odd to me."

"They are blooms, Jonesy, certainly not weeds. I've been helping clear the neglected gardens of the vicarage, and Liam has been doing some of the heavier work."

"Liam, is it? Not Vicar O'Neill . . . or Your Lordship?" Jonesy said with a bow and a snicker, looking around at the others.

"Don't be snide, Jonesy. He asks that people call him Liam," Drew replied.

"And he doesn't 'favor' her," barked Sam. "She was hired to clear those gardens. It's just a job."

"Ha! You are daft, Samuel Provens, if you think the man's not taken with your girl," smirked the conductor. Then he shook his head and laughed all the way out the office door.

After throwing Drew a confused and pleading look, Sam stumbled out of his chair and followed Jonesy. Granda and Drew sat in stiff silence, contemplating what had just occurred.

"I tend to agree with Jonesy, Drew Girl, and I think you know it as well. And might you feel the same toward young Liam? I don't envy your heart's quandary. It is never easy to sort through our choices and decide what might make us content."

The rest of the day at the station passed like a dirge. It was pasta Friday, and they were going to plan and begin preparing dinner for Liam and Theda before they left for Belfast.

At five to the hour, Drew packed up. After carefully placing the large bouquet of pussy willows in her satchel, she began her ride home. Before Jonesy's tirade, she had been excited for the evening with Nonna and Serena, but remembering the look on Sam's face as he ran from the office, she felt guilty and confused.

Because they were making Liam and Theda a dinner of traditional Welsh foods, Drew did not smell the usual fragrance accompanying a pasta Friday. Instead of a rich red sauce simmering on the stove, there was the equally delicious smell of lamb stew.

When Drew entered the door, traditional tunes of Welsh music filled the air as Nonna and Serena danced around the kitchen table, their apron strings flying about them.

"Come join us, Drew Girl! It isn't Italian opera today but the Welsh music of the crwth, fiddle, and pipes. Better dancing tunes than arias."

Drew laughed, washed her hands, grabbed her apron, and joined her favorite women in the world. Her mood lifted as the music of the Welsh folk songs moved them round and round the warm kitchen. When the recording ended, they fell into the kitchen chairs, laughing and out of breath.

"Howard has always told me that songs of love are the most popular theme of Welsh music. He says there are at least 170 songs about love found and love lost," said Nonna, fanning her face with the hem of her apron.

"Well, I expect that is true in all languages in every country of this world," responded Serena, fanning herself as well.

"Love is not a topic I am at all interested in today. I am glad I can't understand Welsh or I would have to say no music for us this evening."

"Ah, Drew. And what happened today to make you so put off love?"

Drew heaved a sighed, then stood up, removed the pussy willows from her satchel, and laid them on the table. She sat again and related all that had happened at the depot, including Jonesy's rude comments.

"So that is the pussy willow incident, and these blooms are evidence of an embarrassing and confusing morning. One I feel both guilty and angry about, and I really don't think I need to feel either. Liam is a friend, and it was thoughtful that he brought the branches to the depot. I really am quite tired of all the drama and emotion. It is exhausting."

"Ie, it certainly is! I feel all of that for you just hearing about this pussy willow incident," said Serena, a compassionate smile on her face.

"I say," began Nonna, standing up, "that we get on with prepping and cooking our dinner for Sunday and let love in all its befuddlement just fly out the door."

Nonna stepped to the door, opened it wide, and said, "Love, be gone with you and don't return until you have wise counsel. Shoo, shoo, begone!"

Looking about the kitchen strewn with an array of ingredients, Drew smiled. "Well, now that love won't be bothering us, I have a few questions. First, how in the world did you find a cut of lamb? And cheese for the rarebit, and butter, sugar, and flour for the Welsh cakes? Where did you get all the extras?"

"Oh, we traded a bit here and there. You never know what someone else may want or need," said Serena. "There is no other way to make anything special if we do not, and certainly, we want the vicar and his aunt to feel special. At this point, I feel like the rationing will never end. In wartime, it felt like we were contributing to the cause, but now, two years later, the rationing has only gotten worse."

"And as for the lamb, well, I can't say how it came to be in the pot any more than I can recall where the extra butter and sugar came from," Serena said with her mischievous grin.

"You know, Serena," said Drew, "you can get heavily fined or even arrested for dealing on the black market."

"Drew! I am deeply offended that you would accuse me of engaging in any illegal activity. Trading and bartering do not need to involve the black market."

"Really, though, you are walking a very fine line," Drew cautioned.

Serena shook her finger at Drew while winking at Naomi. "You worry about your job and your love life, Miss Davies, and your nonna and I will worry about feeding us all."

"I, too, thought by now the rationing would have ended. We are all exhausted by still having to 'make do and mend.' How can we mend without food and jobs, petrol and coal, and adequate housing for our people? Our country is almost bankrupt now that America has stopped their financial help and required we begin paying that help back," lamented Nonna, leaning heavily against her kitchen sink.

She stood with her back to the other women for a moment, then let out a great sigh. When she turned around, her face was set in a determined state of cheerfulness. "Drew, we wrote out the traditional recipes for you to add to your own recipe book."

Five recipes, written on heavy paper, sat in the middle of the kitchen table: lamb stew, laverbread, Welsh cakes, Welsh rarebit, and Glamorgan sausages.

"Of course there are many other recipes for traditional Welsh foods, but these are the ones Granda requested we make and serve this Sunday. Yesterday, he gathered the cockles for the laverbread, purchased the seaweed from one of the fishmongers in town, and presented them to me with great ceremony—his gift to me from the sea, he said. Serena and I started the lamb stew late this morning, and we will reheat it on Sunday. Letting stews and soups sit and then reheating them always improves the flavor. Don't you agree, Serena?"

"Ie. That is also true with Italian soups and sauces. Pasta is best fresh, of course, but we all know that."

Nonna began assembling crocks and pans and all that was needed for preparing the dishes they would finish that evening. "Since the stew has another two hours to simmer, we can start the laverbread and bake the tea cakes. Sunday before dinner we can make the rarebit and Glamorgan sausages.

"Drew, please start the seaweed for the laverbread. It needs several rinsings, then its chopped into small pieces and simmered in water for at least four hours. I'll keep an eye on you, as Granda wants to be sure you know how to make his favorite dish. We'll add olive oil, lemon juice, salt and pepper, and cockles before cooling. Serena and I can start the Welsh cakes. We'll serve those for desert with jam and tea."

"I know that everything we are cooking now is for dinner on Sunday, but what are we having for dinner tonight? I am already more than hungry," said Drew as she cut the washed seaweed into pieces and placed it into the simmering water.

"I brought lasagna. No meat, but the vegetables are just as tasty. I'll put it in now. And I have leftover bread, so you will be well fed. I'm relieved to know your difficult day worrying over matters of the heart has not diminished your appetite. Nothing should come between a woman and good food. Not even love." Serena smiled and winked at Drew.

When dinner was finished, the seaweed for the laverbread was nearly done simmering, and the cockles and spices were added. After helping Nonna and Serena put the kitchen in order, Drew gathered up Vesuvi and her thoughts and went to her room to dream of pussy willows growing amongst the seaweed and both being gathered by two men bearing them as gifts.

CHAPTER 23

COFFEE, CLUES, AND SUSPECTS – SATURDAY, APRIL 12

The night before, Drew had asked Granda if they might sit at the kitchen table the next morning, that she had much to share with him. She woke early and after washing wrapped her cozy robe around her and made her way to the kitchen in search of coffee. Granda was already sitting in his usual place at the head of the table, sipping what smelled like rich, aromatic coffee and reading the newspapers he always shared with her.

"I thought you were planning on sleeping the day away, Drew Girl. I'll get your cup poured."

"It's only seven o'clock, Granda. I need strong coffee and no jesting." She smiled, settling in at her usual place, her back to the hearth. She took the cup that Granda offered and tasted the hot brew. "Wherever did you find this delicious coffee? I hope you have more."

"Henri Reichenbach, of course. I swear that man can get ahold of anything. He assures me he can find more, and I assured him we will appreciate having some from time to time."

Drew saluted Granda with her cup, then opened the leather journal he had given her only a short while ago. She was startled and a little sad to see it so full of notes already.

Granda, guessing her feelings, said, "Ah, don't you worry, there are more small books I will get for you. The recording of all you see, hear, and find are of the utmost importance in an investigation. You can never assume you will remember it all, and memories can become distorted with time, even within hours. He refilled both their cups and sat down again, waiting for Drew to enlighten him.

"Before I tell you all that Lillian and Charlotte found, have you spoken to Inspector Lewis regarding anything that could possibly lead to suspects?"

"The official from the railway spoke with Lewis again two days ago and asked the same question. Lewis told him what we already knew, that the only passengers other than those coming from Ireland were all local residents and frequent commuters. When questioned, none of them appeared to have any connection to Ireland or Eireann Swan."

As they sipped, Drew then related what Charlotte and Lillian had learned regarding Eva and Rex Archer and William Bennett.

"I know everyone that meets Mr. Bennett assumes he is a man of integrity, partly because he is a famous writer and also because he looks the part of a man of unquestionably good character. We know that is not necessarily the case.

"And I do believe that William's daughter Eileen may be somehow involved with the murder. Either as the person who committed the crime or as an accomplice to the person who did. I think she was on the train that day. When I asked her outright if she was, she refused to answer, insisting instead that I was to be done questioning her father about the "murder." To my knowledge, no one knew until two days ago that it *was* murder, and when I told her father several minutes later that it was, he appeared genuinely surprised. Yet, she already knew.

"As a physician, Eileen could have had access to poison, thus giving her means. She also had motive: her mother was another unintended victim of an IRA bombing. The same circumstances in which Eva's father and brother were killed. Even though I do not want to suspect William Bennett, he certainly could also have been an accomplice or the person that served the poisoned tea.

"And what do you make of Eileen's relationship with her father? Are they close?" asked Granda.

"During my time in their home, Eileen appeared to be extremely possessive and protective of him, but he is not a man that appears to want nor need protection. She was also very rude, behavior which her father dismissed and attributed to her ongoing anguish over the loss of her mother. That is a good many years to carry such an angry grief into adulthood. But I know time is not a factor in how long one grieves.

"We can also postulate that Eva Gallagher Archer may be the murderer and acquired the poison either from Eileen Bennett or from another source. Accusing Eva Archer would seem logical not only because she had motive, but perhaps the means as well as the opportunity. It would be convenient to jump to conclusions regarding Mrs. Archer because she is such a disagreeable person. And, of course, her husband may also have been an accomplice." Drew was out of breath from her long dissertation, and she held up her cup for more coffee.

Granda brought the coffee pot to the table. "The way you describe Rex Archer, might he be someone who presents himself one way but is an entirely different person? Say, someone with strong political beliefs hiding behind the guise of an arrogant man of means?" asked Granda, refilling his own cup.

"From all I have observed and learned regarding Rex, I believe he is a man who looks the other way if he sees anything that might disrupt his privileged life, the life of a self-indulgent would-be painter with little else on his mind but 'finding the light.' He seems someone who would also turn a blind eye and sidestep acknowledging actions by others that could place his lifestyle in jeopardy, including the actions of his wife. There seems to be no devoted affection between the two, at least not from what they say of one another. But of course, with his money, he could easily lend support to any political beliefs he may have. Anonymously, at that."

"You have certainly done your homework. You sound like a seasoned detective, Miss Davies. You speak so confidently about what you've found, you could be standing beside the other detectives sharing information.

"But before you narrow the field of suspects to just these four, as you have proposed, let us consider that Eva and Eileen may have plotted together to kill Eireann, and neither Rex nor William were involved at all. Or all four of them could have been in on the scheme and all are guilty. Another possibility is that none of them committed the crime, and the murderer is far away from Mumbles by now."

Drew nodded, saying, "Ie, those are all possibilities, but I would certainly like to rule out any or all of the four suspects we have before moving on; my gut tells me at least one of them is guilty of murder. I am thinking we need to find ways to let these four know that we are aware of their connection and possible motive for Eireann's murder. I have an idea to propose to begin flushing them out.

"Eva Archer visits the library nearly every day with her two children in tow. She says she has nowhere else to go on days they cannot be at the beach. She always makes her entrance about an hour before teatime and insists the librarians prepare her a cup, then rants and clamors when neither Charlotte nor Lillian will do so, repeatedly being told that the library does not offer tea service to *any* library patrons. She then storms out, leaving her well-behaved children behind, and disappears for the next two hours, supposedly in search of refreshment. I was there when this happened, and she made quite a spectacle of herself.

"Her behavior seems like an act to have time to do as she pleases without her children about. Both young Penny and Braden seem very content to be on their own and not the least concerned when their mother leaves them alone to read and just be. They seem quite used to it. So, let's start with Mrs. Archer.

"Since she spends a great deal of time at the library and seems to take it as a personal afront that tea is not served to her when she is there, I think that the library needs to sponsor a ladies Spring Tea next Sunday. I am sure Charlotte and Lillian would be more than happy to sponsor such an event. They could invite and deliver the invitations to myself, Nonna, Serena, and Eva, and perhaps Joanne. With Charlotte and Lillian, that would make seven of us. And, of course, the ladies of the library would have the tables all set up and decorated with name cards indicating where each woman will sit.

"I will be seated next to Eva, who will have a special cup at her setting, a cup matching the one from the train. Charlotte had one exactly like it at the library, one of many from her collection. I want to see Eva's reaction when she picks up the cup identical to the one from which Eireann drank the poison, one made in her father's factory. What do you think?"

"It is quite an elaborate scheme, and if nothing comes of it, you ladies will have had a pleasant tea. I plan to hide and watch," Granda added with a wink.

Drew smiled as she quickly wrote her notes in the journal.

"And Drew, before we leave the table . . ."

Drew froze at the change in Granda's voice and demeanor.

"I want to sit just a few more minutes together," he said, pulling a file from beneath his newspapers. "With all that is going on around us, now may not be the best time, but I know you've been wondering if I have found any more information regarding your parents' death. Lewis and I have done some further digging and secured several documents that I want to show you. I have not found concrete evidence that any foul play was involved, but your father seems to have been engaged in activities that may have put them in danger."

Drew couldn't move. She couldn't speak, but nodded her head to acknowledge she heard him and waited for him to go on. There would never be a "best time" to learn more, but she did want to know.

"Your father joined the army in 1922 and served with the railway battalion for two years. In 1924, he was reassigned, but Marco never told me, wouldn't tell me anything about what he would be doing or where he was going, and I understood not to ask.

"After a time, I wondered if he had been recruited by military intelligence working within MI5. He would come home from time to time, and on one of his returns—this would have been in 1924—he returned with your mother. He and Michela had been quietly married, and she was pregnant with your brother. She was a lovely and personable young woman, and we immediately loved her. She stayed with us when Marco went off to wherever he went, sometimes for a few days, sometimes for a few weeks.

"After this went on for a while, I once again inquired as to what he was involved in. He said to please not question him again, not to worry, and that he was being careful and was not in immediate danger. This told me more than he realized, and that was when I was sure he was involved with an agency such as MI5.

"What did MI5 do? What do you think he was involved in?" asked Drew.

"It was and still is a special operations unit conducting secret intelligence services. After the war, the agents were primarily focused on counterterrorism and espionage within the United Kingdom.

"In the spring of '28, your father told me that he had completed his time in the service and wanted to take up his career on the railway again. I was, of course, relieved that he was out of what I believed to be harm's way and was home for good with his family. Matteo was four by then, and you were two. He came home permanently and got on with the railway, and our lives as a family began to settle down. He never spoke about what he had been doing for those two years before.

"And then, in the fall of that year, they were gone, killed in the automobile wreck. I contacted all the sources I have, Drew, and asked Chief Inspector Lewis to do the same, but we have found nothing further on whether their death was accidental or intentional. I am sorry, Drew Girl, but while I may have my suspicions, as does Lewis, we will never know what exactly happened on that dark road that night."

Granda pushed the open file from which he was reading toward Drew. "Take it and read through it. I think I told you all that is in the document from the records we secured. I don't think it tells the whole story, but this is as much information as we will be given. Larger sections of the documents have been redacted, which tells us there is more to be told that is not being revealed. That information is somewhere else, held in more secure files away from people like us who want answers."

Drew took the file, glancing at what was written but not reading the words. She trusted Granda had told her all that could be said. "Thank you for trying to find out what you could. We have no more answers than before, really, but it does seem Papa served his country and perhaps died because of it. They all died because of it. Maybe it is no different than losing them during wartime, and we can be proud. Not today, but eventually, maybe."

Drew lifted Vesuvi from her lap and set him on the floor, then stood and went to wrap her arms around her grandfather. "I love you, Granda, and my tears are for us all."

She straightened herself and wiped her eyes, as did Howard. "And Granda, I want you to know that I filled out the application for the Passenger Van Guard position and sent it on to the home office in London. I thought it best not to involve you until I had it mailed, just in case anyone asked you if I had applied so you could honestly answer that you did not know."

Howard's response to Drew's news was just a nod of his head as he held up his coffee cup in silent salute to her tenacity. He shared the newspaper with her and they read silently until the library opened.

Drew pulled herself from other thoughts and called to set the wheels in motion for the tea. Charlotte and Lillian were enthused by the idea and said they would get the invitations written and delivered by the next morning and arrange everything at the library. Drew volunteered Nonna and Serena to make Welsh cakes and Charlotte said she would provide finger sandwiches. Lillian insisted on making whatever else was needed for "a proper tea." Drew thanked them profusely and went to get dressed for the day.

The remainder of the day brought some welcome sunshine as Drew helped Nonna with the washing. By noon, they had the clean, damp clothes hung outside on the lines to dry. Later, Drew would iron, loving the aroma of damp cotton as it steamed and sizzled from the iron's hot plate.

They worked in companiable silence, Drew's thoughts on all that Granda had shared this morning. She was glad it was a Saturday and she could be home alone with Nonna. They stopped for lunch before weeding the gardens, tidying the green house, and tending to the chickens and, finally, dusted the cottage and scrubbed its floors. Both women were peacefully content together, carrying on with their domestic tasks.

Their cottage gardens were mostly planted, the vegetables and flowers in the ground waiting for warming sun. Next Saturday, Drew planned to help Liam plant the gardens at the vicarage, but she only had a few seeds and starts from their own pots to take to him. Again, she required help from another front. Finishing her chores by four o'clock, she decided to ring Mara with a suggestion.

"Yes, Miss Davies? Whatever it is you must say, say it quickly, as I am just on my way out."

"This won't take but a minute, Mrs. Roberts. All the gardens at the vicarage are ready to be planted with vegetables and flowers. The problem is we need seeds and plants to put into the ground. I was hoping that you might ask the Women's Auxiliary if they would be willing to donate to the vicarage gardens from their own plots. And if so, could they drop them off at the church this week, and I would pick them up on Saturday morning on my way to the vicarage? I know how you all want to help the new vicar in any way you can, and he has taken an interest in seeing the gardens prosper."

"What a novel idea, Miss Davies. I think I will suggest it to the women myself today. I am just now on my way to our weekly meeting. They will be thrilled when I present the idea of supporting our new clergyman in this way. I believe I can assure you, there will be an abundance of plants and seeds waiting for you on the church steps next Saturday. Nine o'clock. Please don't be late. I really must be going, Miss Davies. Goodbye now."

A WELSH REPAST – SUNDAY, APRIL 13

Granda decided the kitchen was too cold for company coming and built a cozy fire while Drew and Naomi cooked. By six o'clock, between the heat of the fire and the flames from under the simmering food on the stove, their company would step into a cottage full of warm welcome.

Drew oversaw answering the knocks on the door as Nonna and Serena scurried about the kitchen, finishing preparation of the local dishes they would be serving that evening. Granda lingered outside, waiting for his friend Monsieur Reichenbach to arrive.

Liam and Theda arrived at a quarter after the hour, a bottle of something in Liam's right hand and another bouquet of pussy willows in Theda's left. Drew had been keeping an eye out the window and opened the door before they could knock.

"Drew!" exclaimed Theda, giving the girl a tight hug and a kiss to each cheek. Liam didn't seem to know what was expected in way of a greeting to Drew since Theda began hers with a hug as well as kisses. Drew merely smiled at the awkward moment and held her hands out to take the bottle he offered.

"Welcome, and come in where it's warm. We hope you've arrived hungry and with an inquisitive appetite ready to try something new."

"We certainly have," said Liam. "Auntie only allowed us tea and a biscuit for lunch so we could have both a hearty and, as you say, inquisitive appetite this evening."

The kitchen became alive with activity as Theda proceeded directly to Nonna and handed her the bouquet, giving Serena a smile in greeting. Liam stood in front of the hearth while Drew set the bottle of wine on the sideboard and then joined him at the fire. Theda insisted on helping at the stove and was put to business stirring the laverbread and chattering away with the ladies.

"Thank you so much for having us to dinner, Drew," said Liam quietly. "We both looked forward to it all day, and with Auntie Theda leaving tomorrow, this will make her returning home less painful." After a pause, he added with a smile, "It is also very good to see you."

"It is good to see you too. I've so looked forward to having you both with us this evening. I am sorry that your aunt must return to Belfast under such difficult circumstances. Though she does seem in much better spirits than the last time I saw her."

"I agree. She is more of her plucky self. She is a strong woman and capable of handling much, even her grief. I'll be back in Belfast soon to help her as well. I only wish I knew what lay ahead."

"I know what lies ahead for tonight: a great deal of Welsh favorites that you may or may not find tasty." Drew smiled. "Please know that none of us will be offended if it isn't to your liking. I have a strong preference for Italian food and find some of the local traditional fare less than appealing, especially laverbread. I almost hope you don't like it. Then I will not be the only one at the table that can't even abide the smell."

"And you call yourself a Welsh maiden. How very dishonorable of you, Drew Davies. I don't even want to think about how you might malign our Irish fare."

"Now you are being too harsh on me, Liam O'Neill. I could eat my weight in Welsh cakes and rarebit and will certainly enjoy *most* everything else offered tonight. And I would definitely like to try Irish food. Next time your aunt is here, perhaps she can cook for us."

"Oh, she is a fine cook, so you can count on being introduced to several Irish delicacies. And if they are not to your extreme liking, then I cannot tell you what horrendous fate might await you. A lovely colleen cannot live on Italian food alone."

"I like to think my palate is even-handed and can enjoy food of all tastes. At least, most foods." They watched the three women chatting as they moved about the kitchen before Drew said, "I'm going to light the candle on the table, then let's go outside. Granda has been waiting for his friend Henri, and I want to see if he has arrived. Knowing Granda, Henri has been here for some time and they are talking the night away."

Drew and Liam took the single candle and found Granda and another gentleman talking quietly as they walked toward them in the dusky light.

"I think dinner's about to be served, and you two might want to think about coming in to eat. Hello," said Drew, extending her hand to the stranger. "I'm Drew, Howard's granddaughter. I am so pleased to finally meet you in person. And this is my friend, Liam. I should probably introduce him as Vicar O'Neill."

"*Bonsoir* to you both. I am Henri Reichenbach. Your *grand-père* and I met at the Swansea market last year, and since then we have become *bons amis*," said Henri, his French accent delighting Drew's ears.

"And Henri has brought us excellent French wine, which we need to take inside and open." Granda led the way as the four new friends, talking and laughing as they walked, entered the warm cottage.

The three women, all wearing aprons now, were conversing as old friends might while placing platter after platter of food on the table. Nonna set the large pot of fragrant lamb stew in the center and turned to everyone, saying, "It is wonderful to have you all here. Please sit where you would like."

"And as you find your places, I will open the wine our friend Henri has brought us. The goblets on the table are also by benefit of Henri. They were a wonderful discovery last year at his stall at the Swansea market and were a gift for my Naomi after the cottage was ransacked and most everything in the kitchen destroyed."

Nonna and Serena welcomed Henri with hearty greetings and warm smiles.

The wine was opened, and Serena exclaimed, "A tight cork freeing the wine is one of my favorite sounds. My father used to say, 'The louder the pop, the better the wine.'"

Henri added, "And in France, we say that wine enjoyed with friends is a very good wine."

Everyone laughed, and Howard moved from place to place, pouring the ruby-red liquid into each gleaming crystal glass. Nonna, as always, sat to Howard's left, then Serena, and beside her, Theda. Across from Theda sat Liam, and next to him was Drew and then Henri. Drew was glad that Liam was beside her and knew that they both had made certain that was the arrangement.

"I do hope you enjoy this burgundy," said Henri. "Howard told me lamb stew was to be served and this vintage should pair nicely with the meal. There are two bottles so please enjoy."

Howard walked back to his place at the head of the table and looked around at each of the guests. "We are indeed happy to have new friends here today and are mindful as well, Miss O'Neill and Vicar O'Neill, of the grief that has been yours to carry. Let us lift our glasses to family and friends as we remember Miss Eireann Swan."

"To Auntie Eireann," said Liam softly, lifting his glass toward the others and sending Theda a reassuring smile.

There was a reverent silence until Serena spoke up, saying, "Now, Howard, as a full-blooded Welshman, please take us on a tour of the table, introducing our guests to these traditional dishes before us."

Howard named each dish as Nonna chimed in what ingredients went into the making and how it was prepared. "The sausages are called Glamorgan and have resumed prominence during these long years of rationing. They contain no meat but are made from leeks, breadcrumbs, and cheese.

"Hand me your bowls, and I will serve the lamb stew," directed Nonna, reaching across the table for Henri's bowl. "It is too hot to pass from hand to hand."

The stew was ladled and sausages, rarebit, and laverbread made an appearance on each diner's plate. Drew's plate, however, was the one exception, as she did not take even a spoonful of the laverbread. She quietly passed it on to Liam, saying with a smile, "Start out with a small bite."

"Henri," said Serena, "please tell us, where in France do you live and how did you come to find yourself in Wales?"

"I was a peddler with a fine wagon and a finer donkey since my youth, and my father was a peddler before me. When I was growing up, several families, all relatives, lived together side by side. We bought and sold household wares and furniture and farmed some vines and grains on a small plot in northeastern France, along the River Meuse. That is where I have lived all my life and still do today.

"And I understand your grief," Henri lamented, looking between Theda and Liam. "I have recently lost someone in my own life, my dearest friend, Marie. I have a nephew, Felix, and his own family, but I find myself somewhat lost and wandering from place to place, avoiding the memories that linger of the person I most loved. Traveling helps take my mind off what I am missing most at home.

"My travels brought me to the British Isles, through London and southern England and then into Wales. I am very partial to Mumbles and Swansea. How very terrible that the marketplace itself was bombed so heavily in the blitz and must currently make do in such depleted circumstances. And yet, the market carries on, as does life, and I am very happy to be a part of it.

"As I said, I met Howard at Swansea market. I have had a stall there for a short time now, selling wine and antique wares from France, having been a gentleman of commerce since before the Great War.

"I also do business in Paris and London, and travel by ship and train back and forth from these places. It is wonderful to be here this fine evening, with new friends in Mumbles. I, too, live in a village, and your homes and life here are familiar and comforting. I sincerely thank you for having me as your guest."

Liam reached his hand in front of Drew to clasp Henri's arm. "Thank you for your condolences, and we, in turn, are sorry for your own loss. Grief has no timetable and is a cunning, devious emotion. Just as one is beginning to mend, it sneaks up on you unawares and opens the painful wound again." He then added, "But the passing of time does help heal us. Especially as we allow light and life into our lives once again. Tonight is certainly such a time, and we are blessed to be here together."

Nonna looked at Theda. "And Drew tells us you are traveling home to Belfast tomorrow. We will be sorry to see you go so soon."

"Yes, I'll be returning home with Eireann's ashes. I am frightened by how empty life might be there without her beside me. I am not looking forward to walking into the empty house with decades of memories waiting to accost me."

"I'll be joining her on the twenty-second," shared Liam. "The church has granted me a month's absence, and together we will sort things out." He reached across the table to take his aunt's hand. "All will be well, Auntie."

The second bottle of the burgundy was a long while gone, as were the Welsh cakes and jam, when the fire, along with the conversations, began to ebb. Theda set her napkin on the table, saying it was the most delicious stew she had ever eaten. Liam boasted to Howard that he very much enjoyed the laverbread and had two portions, to which Drew rolled her eyes in mock disbelief.

The guests made mention of parting and yet they all lingered over goodbyes. Not just the usual goodbyes, knowing you will see each other again tomorrow or the next week, but a goodbye possibly steeped in forever.

As Drew looked into Theda's sad eyes after giving her a final embrace, she felt bereft at the letting go. The scent of this brave woman's cologne would fade into the evening as she passed beyond the cottage door—as she passed from Drew's life.

And what of Liam? Would his goodbye in a few days' time be forever as well?

Heavy with sad weariness, Drew sat upon the hard chair in the empty kitchen and watched the candle flicker down to a single spark.

CHAPTER 25

WHAT WE OWE – TUESDAY, APRIL 15

The day had gone by so slowly that by the time he could talk to Drew, Sam knew he was riled up. He slowed his fast pace and took a deep breath as he walked into the station office and stood in front of Drew's desk.

"I'm done for the day. Are you almost ready to leave? I thought we could meet at the pier for a bit and just talk. Besides seeing you at the station, we haven't made time to really catch up since we were at my parents.'"

Drew looked up and took a breath, taking in Sam's furrowed brow and fast speech. "Ie, I'm almost ready. Meeting at the pier is a good idea, as we probably have much to catch up on."

"Why don't you toss your bike into my truck, and we'll go down together," said Sam hopefully.

"I still need to finish up with Granda, so you go on ahead. I'll meet you there as soon as I can."

Sam left, looking frustrated as Drew watched after him. Her stomach turned again, thinking of what might be said. She hadn't told him she had applied for the van guard position, but she was sure he knew. And for no good reason she could conjure, she felt pangs of guilt about her confused feelings toward Liam. She slowly put her papers away, went to her grandfather's desk, and quickly kissed him on the cheek.

"All is well, Drew Girl. You just go and have a nice conversation. And keep it honest, always keep it honest."

Sam was standing along the intricately scrolled railing of the promenade looking out over the water. The gulls were calling, flying over and around the lighthouse in the distance, and the sun was still bright in the sky. She leaned her bicycle against the rail and stood beside her friend.

"I don't get down here enough, so I always forget how beautiful it is. I love looking out at the lighthouse. Remember all the times we rowed out there when we were younger?" said Drew.

"Of course I remember. Seems like a hundred years ago." Sam took a breath and exhaled it strongly through his nose. "I understand you've been busy between your job at the depot and working at the vicarage, and now I hear you may be applying for the van guard job."

Drew's gaze stayed fixed toward the island and the lighthouse. "Did you hear that Jonesy gave me a dressing down? Not a woman's place to apply for a man's job and all that."

"Ie, I heard. Everyone heard, and everyone is surprised you're thinking of applying for it."

Drew winced and looked sternly at Sam. "Interesting what makes people shake their heads, make accusations and judgments. Applying for the position is a logical step if I want to continue my railroading career and work hands-on with the trains."

"I guess that's why they're surprised. Why would you want the job? It *is* a man's job. Sure, I know, the women helped during the war years, but that's over and done. The men are back, and the women can be doing their own jobs— being at home with their children and taking care of the house. Doesn't that make perfect sense?" Sam was picking through his words carefully, but glancing at Drew he could see the ire rise in her eyes.

"And you wonder why we haven't spoken? Even though you have promised time and again to support my ambitions? I even believed you meant it."

"I've been thinking about all of it, Drew, and why I wasn't happy to hear you might apply. If it were any other woman, I wouldn't care one way or another. But you're not any other woman. I think of you as mine and that we were meant to have a future together. If you become a guard, I can't see how that would work. You know how hard it is working on the train cars and the engines. The work is physical and the schedules are always changing. How could a woman keep a home and raise children and do that job too?"

"I am young and strong. Certainly stronger than some of the men already working as conductors and guards. I could pick Jonesy up and toss him across the rail yard. And when we talked about this before, I told you I am not ready to marry and certainly not ready for children. Someday I want that, all of it, but not now. Not yet. Now I want to go as far as I can with my dreams."

"And what about all the time you're spending with Vicar . . . whatever his name is? You've been over there after work and on the weekends. That's a lot of time to spend cleaning a house and such."

"Are you implying my actions are somehow inappropriate or are you just jealous? For your information, the Women's Auxiliary hired me to clear and plant the horribly overgrown gardens at the vicarage. We've been working long hours to get those into some semblance of order."

"And who is 'we'? Are the ladies helping or the vicar? I hear it's just you and the vicar. Drew Davies, you have people talking about you for more reasons than you know."

"What I do and who I am with is no one's business but mine."

"Doesn't that seem selfish, that you're only thinking about what you want? Your feelings? What about what I want, what I need?"

"And what you want, Sam, is to settle down? Marry me right now and start a family? Is that what this is about?"

"Ie, I do want that, Drew. I want that more than anything. And it's time."

Drew turned and stood quietly looking at her friend. They both needed to calm down and settle themselves. It was some moments before she said in a gentle voice, "I do understand what you want, Sam, and that you think the time is right. And that may be true for you, but it isn't for me."

Sam reached forward and wrapped his hands around Drew's, watching the breeze blow through her hair. Her loveliness hurt his heart. "What if I say I'll wait till you're ready? Remember last Christmas when I told you I had my eye on a cottage not far from your family's? Well, a writer from Ireland bought it out from under me by offering a full cash payment. Which means I need more time to find us another place. But we could get engaged now, make it official, and by then, surely, you'll be ready to marry me."

Drew gently pulled her hands away. "I can't know when I'll be ready to marry, or to even become engaged. And I don't want that kind of pressure. It's not fair to me, and it certainly isn't fair to make you wait. Besides, I can name several young women who have always had their eyes on you, Sam Provens, and any one of them would be thrilled by your attentions."

"I don't want another woman. I love you, and in my dreams of the future, you and I are together. I see our cottage, our gardens, our babies . . . I see a wonderful life together. Don't you know I'm restless and ready to get on with life? Can you at least give me an idea of how long before you might know?"

"How can I say? Some of that might depend on whether I get the van guard job, or any other job at the railway besides behind a desk. That's as honest as I can be."

"And this is as honest as I can be." Sam suddenly gathered Drew into his arms and kissed her long and tenderly.

Drew finally removed herself from Sam's tight embrace and took a step back. She was terribly upset. "I'm sorry, Sam. I can't talk about this right now."

"Then when can you talk about it?"

"I don't know. I just need to go home." Drew turned, sick at heart, confused and angry, and quickly put distance between them. She felt she was losing her best friend but knew she would never succumb to demands or give in to pressure about making decisions for her own life.

She sensed Sam's urgent restlessness, saw it in his eyes and felt the stress in his body. He certainly did seem to need a change, one that would bring him the contentment that she could not. And although the conversation had been difficult at best, she very much enjoyed the kiss, and that was even more confusing.

CHAPTER 26

A TALK IN THE PARK – THURSDAY, APRIL 17

The post office was located in town, directly across from the waterfront. Joanne Sullivan had inherited, so to speak, the job from her father. He had been postmaster for sixty-five years, and his daughter had worked alongside him handling mail since she was old enough to read and reach the countertop. As an adult, Joanne studied and took the exams necessary to become a postmistress, and like her father before her, she was the eyes and ears of all that happened in the village of Mumbles. She lived her life above the post office and never tired of the expansive view of the bay.

This day, Joanne worked later than usual, sending the remainder of the afternoon's telegraphs. Across the road, the sky over the sea was fading into an orange sunset. As she locked the office door, thinking to go find herself a meal, she heard the roar of a motorbike. Never one to miss watching a motorcycle, she stepped quickly onto the sidewalk to catch sight of it. What she saw was Drew Davies atop the seat. Joanne waved her arms frantically, hoping her friend would see her and pull over.

Drew smiled as she saw Joanne. She coasted to the edge of the sidewalk and turned off the bike.

Joanne walked over and whistled. "You told me your granda got this beauty for you at Christmas, but since you've never made an appearance on it, I was beginning to doubt the truth of it."

"There was finally enough petrol that I've driven it to and from work yesterday and today. It's the best feeling in the world, riding like the wind and feeling like you have no cares at all. She's a marvel, isn't she?"

"Ie, she is, and I would trade you my children, if I had any, for just a ride. I flagged you down for more than a keen look though. I know you said you were planning on talking to the train passengers from Ireland to see if they had any information about the woman that died. I heard two of them talking yesterday, just across the road, and thought you might be interested.

"One was a tall, skinny man about my age with not much pale red hair left to him. He was sitting on the bench just across the road smoking a cigarette while a woman with long dark hair, slightly younger it seemed, stood in front of him, pacing and talking loudly. She was clearly angry with him. At one point, he threw his lit cigarette at her, which hit her in the chest. She jumped with a yelp, spun around, and started walking away, but he went after her, grabbed her by the arm, and turned her back around."

"Could you hear what they were saying? Anything at all?" asked Drew.

"Ie, I did indeed. I took a chance, and while she was walking away and he went after her, I quickly ran across the road and stood behind a tree." Joanne grinned. "Sounds just like in the movies, doesn't it? Anyway, when he caught up with her, he said, 'You're not going anywhere. I wasn't the only one involved in this, and you need to remember that.'

"The woman stopped and seemed calmer. She looked at him and said, 'It didn't need to be this complicated. And now it's all gone sideways.'

"The man seemed angrier than before, got right up into the woman's face, and said, 'Don't play the innocent with me, Eileen. You were in from the beginning. You knew there were complications and you said you could handle them.'

"'And I have handled them, but what I can't handle, Rex, is your ruthless need for revenge. Just leave me alone.' Then she turned and walked slowly away.

The man walked back and sat down on the bench, lit another cigarette, leaned his head back, and smoked like he didn't have a care in the world. I thought that was really strange. Like he was glad to have her gone."

"He well could have been, Joanne. He's not the feckless painter that he purports to be, with too much money and time to travel the world for 'the light.' Maybe he had so much of both he planned a murder."

"So what I heard was helpful? Do you think the two of them were in cahoots and killed that woman?"

"It certainly bears looking into. Thank you, Joanne. I owe you a fast ride on my bike."

Drew left Joanne outside her post office and arrived home in time for dinner. She was quiet and far away with her thoughts, never contributing to their usual lively conversation throughout their evening meal. She told her grandparents she was tired, needed to make some notes, and would go to her room right after eating. They shooed her away and took care of the kitchen clean up as she gathered up Vesuvi and headed to her bedroom.

Sitting on her bed, pen in hand, she made copious notes, going over and over what she knew of each person she had spoken with, the conversation Joanne heard, and how they all might be connected with Eireann. Knowing sleep might be hard to find, it was well past eleven before she eventually turned in and tried to settle her mind.

Her sighs and moans of sleepless frustration accompanied by restless tossing and turning finally drove Vesuvi from the bed and into the sitting room. Hearing his loud thump as he jumped to the floor caused Drew to sit up and turn on the nightstand lamp.

She refused to look at the clock, knowing full well she had never been to sleep. Her mind turned over and over as she tried to fit the stubborn pieces of the murder into something that made sense. What did Rex and Eileen's heated conversation at the park mean? Did they orchestrate the murder and carry it out? Was Eva innocent after all, knowing nothing about why Eireann had been killed? And William Bennett? Did he know that Eileen was indeed on the train that day? Did he know his daughter and Rex Archer conspired in some way with each other? Was Bennett also involved in the plotting of her death?

In addition to all these questions, others were vying for equal attention. Did she love Sam . . . really love him? When she replayed all he had said to her, mostly what she felt was guilt . . . and fear. Was she afraid that if she allowed herself to accept a life with him, she might lose him, as she had others she had loved? Could that be why she was so hesitant to commit to him? Even if that were true, she *had* been honest about not wanting to get married right now, or even in the foreseeable future. But could she not consider his offer of becoming engaged and giving her the time she needed?

And what of her confused feelings for Liam? How was it possible, in such a short time, to have such strong feelings for a man she knew so little about? The puzzle of her own heart was more difficult to solve than murder.

PLANTING THE GARDENS – SATURDAY, APRIL 19

Drew arrived on time to pick up whatever plants and seeds Mrs. Roberts was able to cajole away from her women of the auxiliary. Drew had borrowed the lorry again, and two buckets were once again filled with gardening implements and an ample lunch for Liam and her.

As soon as she turned the corner, Drew could see the boxes covering the front steps of the church, all filled with shrubs and plant starts of many varieties. These women really were quite something. She also saw that Eira Hughes was standing beside Mara. It was a surprise to see the sister of the former vicar, someone she had not come across in all the months since her brother was murdered. The auxiliary women must be such a strong support for her and, watching Eira talking with Mara today, Drew could see some life once again returned to the woman.

"You are a tad late, Miss Davies, but we still have time to get this all into your lorry before we must be off."

Drew acknowledged their good morning with her own hello and stepped to the back of the lorry to lower the gate. The three women carried box after box, placing them carefully into the bed.

"How wonderful to see all the lovely plants for the vicarage gardens. I can see I'll be busy through the weekend. In a month's time, the gardens should begin to look amazing. I am sure Vicar O'Neill will be grateful to you all, as he has said the gardens are important to him."

"And grateful he should be. My ladies gave up their own plants for the good of the church. We certainly hope you can keep them up, Drew. It would be a great loss if they were neglected and didn't thrive. And you do plan to keep them up, do you not? Since the vicar doesn't require you to do any meal preparation, in exchange for the same wages you will do the housekeeping twice a week and maintain the gardens. Are we still in agreement?"

Drew set her mind and responded, "I did very simple meal preparation for Vicar Hughes. It took only a short time to lay out his breakfast and prepare a light lunch. The gardens, however, as they go completely around the house, will take hours each week. Therefore, I am asking that I be compensated an extra twenty-five percent in weekly wages."

"Well, Miss Davies, that is quite a bold demand and a surprising one at that. I will need to speak with the church board to see if we have sufficient funds to accommodate what might be considered an unreasonable request."

"It is very reasonable, Mrs. Roberts. My family has gardens as well, and my grandmother and I spend hours each week tending to them. I know how long it takes to care for growing things: planting, weeding, pruning, harvesting, and then there is the canning at the end of it all. I will not be doing the canning, as I am sure the ladies would be more than happy to complete the season in that way. But, again, my asking for an increase of twenty-five percent to ensure the vicarage gardens are a point of pride for the church is very reasonable."

It appeared that Eira set her mind as well. "I agree with Miss Davies, Mara. Those gardens were neglected and an eyesore for all the years my brother lived there. For whatever reason, he would not allow them to be touched, not by any of us. I don't think he wanted anyone around the house, and he certainly wasn't a gardener himself. I like to think the gardens will be, as Miss Davies says, a point of pride for the vicarage, part of a new beginning. So much has been done to make the house lovely and the gardens are an extension of the property. You have my vote, Miss Davies."

Eira Hughes was out of breath when she finished her speech of support. She took a stand against Mara, and Drew could see she was proud of herself. Her aura had grown brighter as she spoke. Adjusting her hat, Eira picked up another box and carried it to the lorry.

"Well, I can't promise anything, but we'll look into it and get back to you," said Mara as she stood watching Drew and Eira finish loading the truck.

Drew bade them both farewell, stepped up into the driver's seat, and drove the short distance to the vicarage. She knew she would get the additional money and smiled that she had made such a "bold demand."

Liam and Rudy were waiting for her when she pulled up outside the white fence. Rudy ran to her with his ever-present red ball in his mouth, bumping up against her in welcome.

"By the looks of the back of this truck, the women plowed up their own gardens," said Liam, grinning.

Drew laughed. "Let's walk the beds again and decide where it all goes."

Liam followed her as they circled the property. They stopped at each garden bed where Drew talked about where to plant what.

"We want the sunny front gardens to be colorful and full of bright flowers, and the flowers and plants that need part shade can go on the north side. The vegetables also need sun, so those will go on the south side and in the back to the west. I see the ladies also included some flowering shrubs, and we can put most of those on the north as well. The heather, azaleas, and rhododendrons will do well there. Fall is usually the best time to plant them, but it is early spring and cool enough that they should do fine. I do wish we had some lavender to put under the front parlor windows.

"You are taking this all very seriously, Miss Davies, and I must say I'm quite impressed with your gardening expertise. Seeing the gardens at your own home, I have realized you do know about that of which you speak."

"You flatter me, Vicar O'Neill. But, yes, I do want the gardens to be spectacular and for you to have vegetables that would win prizes. We can fertilize the soil with donations from my chickens. Let's lay everything out in front of the beds where it will go into the ground. If we work efficiently and late into the evening, I think we can get most everything planted."

"Tomorrow's message to my congregation is typed and waiting on my desk, so Rudy and I are free to play in the dirt with you the entire day."

Liam carried nine small pots of shrubs—three heathers, three rhododendrons and three azaleas—around to the north side of the house and then took what Drew informed him were several different varieties of tomato plants to the sunny west side. Drew was thrilled when she saw the women had put tulips and daffodil bulbs and dahlia tubers into burlap bags, tying them at the top with twine. Many of the bulbs bore beginning stems, and Drew was hopeful they would continue to grow and bloom this spring. She would plant them all and knew that if not this year, then next spring they would make a beautiful blanket of color.

There were sealed envelopes of seeds, each packet marked with what awaited inside: sweet peas, alyssum, nasturtiums, cornflowers, cuckoo flowers, milkmaids, and foxglove. Some packets were unmarked, and those would be a surprise. There were also boxes of just-budding petunias, Snowdon lilies, primroses, black-eyed Susans, and lupine. All of this bounty she placed on the grass before the front beds. How beautiful these beds would be as you walked up the path to the house.

Another burlap bag held potatoes to be divided and planted, onion sets, plus seeds of corn and green beans. Lastly, she pulled a wooden box down that held divides of rhubarb, leeks, and starts of squash plants.

"I really didn't think the ladies would find enough to share that would fill all of these spaces, but this is truly a bounty they have given you."

"I am very much out of my depth. Without you, all these wonderous plants and mysterious seeds would just wither and die. You are the magician that will create all the life that each specimen has to offer. Interesting that each living thing needs to be planted in just the right place to thrive and grow. And to be tended and nurtured all along the way. Hmm, this is a great analogy for each person entering our world."

"Sounds like next week's sermon, Vicar O'Neill."

"You know, tomorrow will be my last sermon here, at least for a while. I only just arrived, and I can hardly believe the terrible tragedy that forces me to leave. I know Auntie Theda is desperate for me to be in Belfast to help her make decisions as well as provide her with some comfort, but truthfully, I don't want to leave."

"You sound serious and sad, Liam. I can't imagine anyone wants you to leave. Especially since you haven't said when you will return."

"So much will depend on my aunt. I have a tentative plan, but I don't know if she'll be willing to make changes. As soon as I know, you and my congregation will be the first to hear of it. The church board has given me a month's leave to decide what I will do. I believe that is generous, and they have expressed the hope that I will be back in four weeks' time." Liam paused and looked about the place, then gazed out to the sea. "I think I could be very happy here."

"I do hope that whatever you must decide makes you happy, your aunt as well. It's a very difficult time for the both of you. Having you in Belfast with her will make it easier to come to decisions that move both of your lives forward." Drew spoke with so much more composure and confidence than she felt.

Hearing Liam's disappointment in having to leave Mumbles made her own greater. The degree of sadness she felt caught her off guard, and she was again confused by her strong feelings of attachment toward this man. And making the day even more unsettling, the tumultuous feelings from her conversation with Sam last evening flooded through her again.

If she just kept herself focused on the planting, she might get through the next many hours. She was on the verge of tears and kept her eyes on the dark soil of the waiting garden beds, moving her small hoe back and forth, back and forth to loosen the dirt. She needed to stay positive and pull herself together.

Handing Liam a long-handled shovel, she settled herself and said, "Alright, let the digging begin. Let's go around back, and I'll show you how deep and wide a hole to dig for the shrubs, just the heather, rhododendrons, and azaleas. We'll plant the hydrangeas on the end of the front gardens, one each side of the entrance. There will be one left to plant beside the front steps. Ready?"

"Aye aye, Captain! Willing, able, and at your service!" Liam perched the shovel over his shoulder and followed her to the back of the house, where they chose places for the large shrubs. After he dug all six holes, Drew had him crawl under the dark underbelly of the house and bring up two long, cobwebbed garden hoses. He screwed one into the spigot on the back wall of the house, and the other one would go up to the front.

After much screeching and moaning, brown water finally emerged from the long hose. "Fill each hole with water," said Drew, "and then we'll place the ball of the shrub into the hole. I'll hold it square while you shovel in the dirt and tamp it down with your boots. Then we'll water it one more time for a good start."

Liam did as instructed, and soon they moved to the back of the house, the west side, to plant the tomatoes, corn, and potatoes. The onion sets, squash, beans, carrots, leeks, and rhubarb they planted on the south side. The beds running along the back and south length of the house were wide enough to accommodate two rows of plants, front to back.

It was one o'clock by the time they finished, and after giving everything a final watering, including themselves, they were tired and hungry. The only beds remaining were on each side of the front walkway, where they would plant the flowers, both seeds and plants.

"Did I see a basket of food in the seat beside you, Drew? My stomach is growling, and my back is aching. I need food and to sit myself down for a rest."

"Ie, you did see lunch and, ie, we both need that rest. Let's go inside. Rudy must be desperate wondering why we haven't checked in on him."

Liam smiled. "He is desperately wondering why he can't be out here helping us plant. He is very good at digging holes, you know."

"That is a worry, Vicar O'Neill. That big dog of yours could destroy all these plants and our hard work in a matter of minutes. I am still thinking about fences."

"We can think while we eat. I hope you brought enough for a hungry man who will give a few bites to his undernourished dog."

"You'll see there is plenty. We need to reenergize so we can work all afternoon."

"Are you sure you weren't an army general in another life? I never could have imagined gardening to be such strenuous work."

"What? You think women's work is easy? Gardening, cleaning, cooking, canning, washing, hanging, hauling, scrubbing, and taking care of a home and children? Men never seem to appreciate the domestic side of a woman's world. They seem to think it happens by magic. And even when women hold jobs, they are still expected to do everything to keep up the home and family. That is why I am in no hurry to leave my job and pursue marriage and more responsibilities. Did I tell you I applied for a passenger van guard position?"

"I do recognize and appreciate how hard women work, many times holding a family together all on their own. Remember, I was raised by two of those strong women," said Liam as they headed up the front steps, the heavy lunch basket between them. "Let's go inside and eat, and you can tell me about the new job."

While Drew laid a platter of rolls with thick cheese on the table, and a small plate of sliced meat with pickled carrots and onions, Liam poured them tall glasses of cool water, gathered plates, forks, and two napkins, and placed it all onto the table.

Settled at the table, passing food between them, Liam asked, "This guard position, is it dangerous? Is it the job of your dreams? Do you see yourself forsaking having a family for your career?"

"You ask a lot of questions and I thank you for that. The answer to the first is yes and no. It can be somewhat dangerous if you were a person who was not mindful of what they were doing. You could suffer a fall and have fingers and limbs impinged. I'll be climbing on and off the trains, hanging out the doors, and sometimes carrying out tasks such as lifting, that require strength. There are a set of job duties along with paperwork. Some of the duties I am already doing. And then there is the fact that you do what needs doing in the moment.

"Secondly, it is the job on the way to my ultimate goal. I want to be an engine driver. That may be unattainable in the foreseeable future, but dreams are like that. And third, another dream is to definitely have a family of my own one day. I do not see why a woman must choose between having a career or a family. Men certainly have both. And women all during wars have done both. I am young, smart, strong, and determined. I believe I can do anything I set my mind and heart to. Does that answer all your questions, Vicar O'Neill," said Drew with a smile and a mouthful of pickled onion.

Liam was smiling as well and nodding his head as he swallowed. "I don't believe I have ever met a young woman quite like you, Miss Davies. At first sight, one would think you but a beautiful young woman who had a way with a rake and a hoe. On closer observation, they would know you are a determined and passionate woman looking into a bright future. I applaud your ambition, your spirit, and your heart."

"Thank you, Liam. I truly mean that. Not everyone feels the same. Certainly, Jonesy and Sam, all the men, and probably most of the women at the station have quite a different opinion of women wanting to work on the trains . . . or working outside the home at all.

"I think Granda understands and would be more vocal in his support but because he is the station master, he can't comment on my applying for the position. Anyway, I won't hear for a while whether I have the job, and I do know others have applied, including Jonesy's nephew. Who, from what I hear, is frightfully underqualified. But time will tell."

"I wish you all the best, Drew, and know that you would be wonderful in anything you set your keen mind to. You must write and tell me how it all turns out."

The reminder that Liam would be leaving put a knot in Drew's stomach, and she began gathering up the remains of lunch. "Back to work, young man. We dedicated gardeners can't sit idle while seeds and flowers await their planting."

They spent the remainder of the day talking and laughing about all sorts of things as the seeds and flowers were put into the ground. They finished with the placement of the three hydrangeas and called an end to their work for the day. While Drew watered the front and side beds, Liam loaded the lorry with the empty boxes, sacks, and the bucket of gardening tools and gloves. They washed their faces and hands and took one last long drink of water from the hose before Liam walked her to the lorry.

"I know you will be busy all day tomorrow, Liam. I hope all goes well at church as you say your goodbyes. I won't be there, but I will come here to be sure everything in the beds looks well, and I'll water anything that looks like it needs another drink."

Liam nodded in agreement, saying, "And you told me tomorrow at one o'clock you have the tea at the library. The outcome will be on my mind, and perhaps we might meet up on the pier later in the day, say at six?"

"Depending on what happens at the tea, meaning if I can get away, I will plan to be at the pier. I would like that very much. Thank you for such a productive and enjoyable day. The gardens really will be wonderful."

"The thanks go to you, Drew. I look forward to seeing you tomorrow."

Liam opened the door of the lorry and Drew hopped in. As she drove away with a backward glance at the young man with dirt on his face and a big ruddy dog at his side, her heart twisted, another dream on her mind.

CHAPTER 28

TEA IS SERVED – SUNDAY, APRIL 20

Spring Tea at the Oystermouth Parish Library
You are cordially invited to the
First Annual Oystermouth Library Spring Tea
Date: Sunday, 20 April
Time: 3:00 pm
RSVP: Charlotte or Lillian at the library

"You have such lovely cursive script, Lillian. I am quite excited about our tea. Even if nothing of interest regarding the murder spills forth, we may be creating what will become an annual event for our little library."

"Thank you, Charlotte, but let us not get ahead of ourselves. Perhaps no one will attend. I do hope, for Drew's sake, that most everyone will be there."

"I think she is giving all but Mrs. Archer an idea of what may occur and encouraging them to attend. Maybe it will indeed be just tea with acquaintances, but then again, perhaps a revelation sparked by a teacup."

"The invitations are all finished. Let's walk to the post office and be sure Joanne gets them out today."

When Drew walked into the library at two o'clock on Sunday, she could hardly believe what she saw. Charlotte and Lillian had transformed the large main room into a beautifully decorated tearoom. A long table had been created and covered with a tapestried cloth in shades of pale yellows and greens. China teacups planted with small single pink and yellow primroses were scattered down the middle amidst tiered silver serving platters. The table was set with silver flatware and matching bone china luncheon plates, and to the upper right of each plate was a teacup with saucer. None of the teacups was matching, instead each unique and lovely. Names on small place cards, written in Lillian's fine hand, indicated where each woman was to sit. Eva Archer was to sit between Drew and Charlotte, the matching teacup from the train at her setting.

After walking around the beautifully laid table to identify where the other women would be seated, Drew walked to the back room, where she found Charlotte and Lillian busy with the assembling of small triangle sandwiches, pastries, and scones. Drew added Nonna's Welsh cakes to the bounty as Lillian asked, "Drew, can you please go gather the tiered plates and bring them here so they can be filled?"

Drew did as asked and then stood watching as the two women delicately arranged the foods in identical fashion onto the tea plates. Lillian placed Nonna's Welsh cakes and small scones on the middle tiers. On the bottom, largest tiers, Charlotte arranged small crustless triangle sandwiches of egg, some of what looked like a pâté of some sort on dark bread that Drew could not identify, and lastly, what looked like chopped chicken with something green. She wasn't sure of the fillings but knew it all smelled and looked divine. Lastly, Charlotte placed slices of apple and cheese on the smallest top tier. Drew's mouth watered as she thought she could probably eat an entire plate on her own.

By two-thirty, the table was laid, and Drew wished they had a camera to capture how lovely everything looked. "Have the two of you created high teas before? This all looks as if it were catered by a London restaurant."

Charlotte and Lillian smiled with pride and said they had been looking at books and magazines to gather ideas.

"And I think we both agree that it looks as marvelous as if we were at high tea at Claridge's, in the Foyer and Reading Room," said Charlotte, giving Lillian a sideways embrace.

At two forty-five, Lillian stationed herself by the door to welcome the guests. Joanne was first to arrive, and Lillian directed her to some chairs set to the side where coats were to be placed. Nonna and Serena were next.

Drew kept one eye on the door, waiting for Eva to appear and, when she did, made a beeline to her side. She took Eva's arm and moved her toward the others so that her back was to the table and she wouldn't spy her place before they were ready to sit down.

Eva was attired in a beautiful cream-colored dress with a cowl neck and dark brown buttons down the front. The skirt fell to her mid-calf and was cut on the bias, allowing the material to swirl around her. The handbag she carried and her leather shoes were the same deep brown as the buttons. On her head was a small round straw hat of bright teal with a single matching feather tucked into the side.

The other women, all dressed in well-worn clothes but also looking lovely, greeted Eva cordially. Everyone agreed that she looked beautiful. The kind attention immediately put Eva at ease as Drew wondered if Theda had made such lovely hats and if this one could possibly be one of hers.

Charlotte and Lillian were wonderful hostesses, and at just a little after three, Lillian cleared her throat and raised her voice slightly to say, "Charlotte and I, on behalf of our wonderful Oystermouth Library, welcome you all. We are having a small gathering today, as we did not know how our afternoon soiree would be received and are so happy that all of you accepted the invitation.

"Please take a seat where you find your name. We shall commence bringing out the tea pots and then you may begin serving yourselves from the trays nearest your seat."

The women chatted as they found their places, and Charlotte and Lillian set three large teapots upon the table. Each pot was covered with a spring-themed crocheted cozy. Drew wondered if the large teapots belonged to them or if they secured them from some treasure trove.

As Eva pulled out her chair, Drew did the same, and they both sat. Eva looked round the table as she slowly pulled off her linen gloves and placed them into her handbag before laying the napkin across her lap. Drew took the opportunity to ask about her children and what they had all been doing since last she saw them.

"Our usual, which is nothing of interest. The only one of us that seems to be getting anything accomplished is Rex, and the only time we really see him is when it rains, as he cannot paint. The children seem more content than I am, playing endless card games and reading countless books. I just want to leave and get on with things." Mrs. Archer said all of this without once glancing toward Drew but looking curiously from woman to woman around the table as she spoke, as though wondering why in the world anyone thought she might enjoy their company.

It wasn't until Charlotte paused at Eva's side to pour her tea that Drew caught Eva's astonished expression as the woman's eyes were drawn to the teacup beside her plate. Drew heard Eva's quiet gasp of recognition and the quick settling of her surprise. Eva kept her hands in her lap and sat perfectly still as Drew said to Charlotte, "The aroma of the tea is wonderful. What is the blend?"

"It is a tea from Belfast that I have often enjoyed. I hope you both do as well."

Charlotte went on to the next woman as Drew asked Eva, "I did not know that there were such wonderful teas in Belfast. What are some of your favorites, Mrs. Archer?"

Eva took some time before clearing her throat and responding. "I only drink traditional English teas. There is nothing in Ireland, much less its tea, that holds any interest for me."

Drew lifted her cup and took a large sip of the tea. "Please do try it, as I think you will find it an interesting blend. You might find your teacup of interest as well."

Rather than pick up the teacup from her family's company, Eva helped herself to a sandwich of egg and one scone. "I think this is all I need at the moment." Eva's tea sat untouched, and Drew saw that the woman's hands were shaking slightly as she picked at her food.

Charlotte came round with tea again. "Mrs. Archer, is the tea not to your liking? Would you like me to pour you another cup?"

"As a matter of fact, yes. And please bring me a new teacup as well and then pour tea again, an English blend this time."

"Of course," said Charlotte, picking up the cup. In a mere moment, as she and Drew had planned, knowing that the teacup might be shunned, Charlotte placed an identical teacup beside Mrs. Archer's plate and began pouring fresh tea.

"I specifically requested another teacup and you have brought me the same one. You must have another, so please get it for me."

"Unfortunately, this is the last teacup we have, identical to the original one at your setting. They are quite special, are they not, Drew?"

"They really are, and made by your father's company, Mrs. Archer. Interestingly enough, I found the exact cup that was just placed before you on the train the day Eireann Swan was poisoned."

As Charlotte walked away, Eva turned to Drew. "What is this ruse, Miss Davies? I have been ambushed and it is immensely upsetting."

Drew leaned toward the woman, saying in a quiet voice, "I can only imagine how upsetting it was for Eireann Swan once she realized the tea she had just been served and consumed contained poison, and she knew she was being murdered."

"I have never heard such an outlandish accusation," Eva said in an even tone, practiced at keeping her self-control. "Are you accusing me of something, Miss Davies?"

"You are an acclaimed actress, Mrs. Archer. You know how to disguise yourself and to appear as a portly gentleman employee of the railway. We found the padded clothes you hid in the lavatory at the depot after you made a hasty exit off the train to then reappear in the lobby and sit quietly with your family. The teacups I found in the carriage are not railway issue but from Gallagher and Son, Ltd., your father's factory. We know he and your brother were killed in an IRA bombing in Belfast, and we know where you most likely secured the poison. That is why you talked your husband into coming to Wales for 'the light.' It wasn't his idea, but yours."

Eva listened in silence until Drew finished reciting what she believed to be evidence against her, then picked up the teacup and drank it to the bottom. "Do all the ladies know that there was a reason for this primitive 'Easter Tea' other than just eating terrible sandwiches and drinking inferior tea?"

"Yes, Mrs. Archer, they are aware."

"Well, Miss Davies, as you say, I am indeed a great actress, and once these ladies finish their chatter, I will give them the greatest performance of my life."

Ten minutes passed as the women finished eating and were all served another cup of tea. Eva Archer then cleared her throat loudly and all eyes turned to her.

"I understand that you have all been let in on the real reason for this little party and were hoping that I might fall to the floor in tears of denial, wailing of my innocence and calling for my solicitor. I am, however, made of stronger stuff. Miss Davies has suggested that I was the one that placed poison in Miss Swan's tea and then served it to her on the train, disguised as a rotund man, a railway employee."

Eva paused there, sighed, and looked at Charlotte. "May I please have an entire pot of tea, English tea, placed in front of me? I have a story to tell, and I will need reinforcement."

Charlotte did as requested. Once the tea was poured in her father's cup, Eva took a long drink, a very deep breath, settled back into her chair, lifted her chin, and spoke.

"I will begin my story from where my life ended, on the day my father and older brother died in an explosion in Belfast that destroyed my father's business and our lives. My father was everything to me, my hero and my protector. I was turning eighteen that week, and Father was taking me to London, just he and I, to celebrate. He had tickets to the Prince of Wales Theatre, and we were to stay three nights in Piccadilly, seeing the sights. Before we were to return home, Father had planned a tour of the university I would be attending come fall.

But all those plans, all of my life was shattered in mere moments by explosives ignited by terrorists.

"Mother took to her bed. She had always been an angry and spiteful woman, and now she completely turned her back on me. Left me to my own devices to find a way to survive. She said there was no money for university, and it was foolish of me to have even considered I needed the same education as her beloved son, my dead brother. I knew she was grieving as well. My brother was adored by her as I was by our father. It never occurred to either of us, in our shock and grief, to perhaps turn to one another for solace.

"The first months after they were killed, I was completely undone, unable to right myself in any fashion. Then my anger consumed me, and I was hell-bent on finding out who destroyed my world. I began to gather all the information I could regarding what happened that day.

"I learned there were witnesses to the bombings, people on their way home at dusk, that spoke of seeing three people at the back of the building. Two men dressed in black and a woman wearing a brown knit cap and high boots. Two people swore they saw the woman ignite the line of dynamite and run from the site. First the explosion, then the end of my life. The woman was chased and run down by those bystanders and, in the midst of all the chaos, subdued until the authorities caught up and arrested her. She was questioned but later released for 'lack of evidence.' Other witnesses could not confirm that this was indeed the same woman that struck the match and lit the flame.

"I read every newspaper, tabloid, and magazine article I could find about the bombing and the ongoing investigation. The IRA had quickly claimed responsibility for the bombing, but the police said there continued to be no evidence directly linking the suspect they first questioned to having played any role in the actual bombing. The suspect's name was Eireann Swan, and she had ties to both the IRA and Cumann na mBan. I knew it was her, just as I knew those 'other witnesses' who said they could not confirm her identity were planted by the IRA to cause confusion so that she would be released.

"But now I had a name. I found out the woman worked in a millinery shop.

My mother no longer needed her car, as she never again went outside the house, so I began driving to the millinery shop, watching who went in and out. It didn't take long to know that only two women worked the store. After a few weeks of watching them and their customers come and go, I took one of my hats in, asking for new feathers.

"'Good day,' I said. 'Who would I speak with regarding replacing the feathers on this hat? Is that something you do here?'

"'I am Theda O'Neill, owner of this shop. I design all of our hats and of course we do refurbish them as well. Would you like to see the feathers I have in stock?' And as we looked at feathers, I was waiting for the other woman to make an appearance, but she never did. I decided on peacock feathers, as she thought they would look handsome, and she told me the hat would be ready in a few days. I told her I might not be back for a week or so. I had previous engagements, and if she could hold the hat for me that would be most appreciated. She said of course.

"I waited two days and then again drove each day to the shop, waiting for a time when the owner left and the other woman remained. On the fourth day, Miss O'Neill stepped from the store, got into her automobile, and drove away. I had seen Eireann Swan enter the store earlier, so I knew she was still inside. I sat for a few moments trying to compose myself before stepping into the presence of the person who destroyed my life.

"'Hello!' I called as I entered the shop. A thin, wiry woman I guessed to be in her twenties came from behind a curtain to the front counter. 'Good day. How may I help you?'

"I nearly flew at the woman, wanted to strangle her thin neck and be done with it. But I steadied myself, took a breath, and said calmly, 'I'm picking up a hat that Miss O'Neill refreshed for me. I believe it must be ready.'

"'Your name please? I'll check and see.' I gave her my name and saw no sign of recognition or panic on her face, but of course, why would she, as she had never set eyes on me before that day. She disappeared behind the curtain and in the few moments she was gone, I struggled to find a way to strike up a conversation, a way to encourage her to talk about herself.

"'I found your hat, and the feathers look lovely. Is there anything else I can help you with today?'

"'I find your shop very appealing. How long has it been here? Do you create hats as well as the owner?'

"She told me how long the shop had been there, and no, she did not make hats. She kept the accounts and handled the business side of things. She wasn't overly forthcoming, but neither was she rude. Just very matter of fact. She wrapped my hat in layers of thin paper, tied it with twine, and handed it to me, telling me what I owed. Placing the coins into her outstretched hand, I remember thinking they would surely burn her palms from my hatred.

"I went away disappointed. I realized I had expected to detect some evil in her or that some rabid political rhetoric would spew from her mouth. I sat in the car and cried, my unassuaged fury drowned in tears.

"I never wore the hat again but kept it propped on my dressing table mirror, reminding me that there would come a time and a way to exact revenge. I just needed to wait.

"And wait I did, going every few months or so to buy a new hat or have one updated, each time being sure Miss Swan was the one I spoke to. She was never any more talkative than the first time I met her and seldom made eye contact. One time, I went to the shop and the other woman, Miss O'Neill, was alone. When I asked for Miss Swan, she told me she was off visiting her family and would be back in two weeks. I went home that night and, as I often did, laid in bed plotting ways to kill the woman. I devised many such methods and wondered which one would win out.

"I am an avid reader of the newspapers, and this last April there was a notice that a Vicar Liam O'Neill was leaving his interim posting at the local Anglican church in Belfast, accepting a permanent posting in Mumbles, Wales. His aunts, Theda O'Neill and Eireann Swan, were planning a small send off after church services on the last Sunday in February. The community was invited to attend. Vicar O'Neill would be delivering the sermon that Sunday.

"Of course, I attended that service and stayed for the send-off. I sought out Miss Swan and Miss O'Neill. They both recognized me from the shop and said they didn't realize I was a parishioner at the church. I said I was, but only occasionally attended services and that I thought their nephew was a gifted speaker. I gushed about how proud they must be of him but also how sad it must be for them that he was moving so far away.

"Miss O'Neill shared that they were traveling to Mumbles by train just before Easter to be sure Liam was all settled into his new place and to take part in his first service, Easter service, as the new vicar. I asked when they were departing, as I wanted to be sure I brought a hat in before they left. They gave me the date, and I left that church, my heart pounding loudly. Rex had been saying that he wanted to go to the south coast of Wales to paint, and now I would make that possible.

"That night, I suggested to Rex that going to Wales for Easter would be a wonderful time to visit the coast. He was, of course, surprised I had shown any enthusiasm at all for his art, much less agreeing to travel to someplace I considered cold and boring. He quickly agreed before I changed my mind. I told him I would take care of all the arrangements. I spent the next weeks honing my plan, gathering what I needed to carry it out, making the rail reservations and securing our rooms at the B and B, and, finally, finding and padding the uniform for my disguise. I was prepared for what was possibly the last performance of my life. And when I saw Eireann Swan drink that cup of revenge, I knew all those weary years of waiting had been worth it. She was guilty of murder and I punished her. I am guilty of her murder and will gladly accept my own punishment."

Eva Archer sat back in her chair, took a deep breath, and exhaled long and slowly. "You know the rest, and I am tired of talking and would like another pot of tea, please."

As Lillian poured more tea into everyone's cups, Drew said, "I have a question, Mrs. Archer. Did your husband know anything of your plans to kill Miss Swan?"

"Of course not. Why in the world would I tell him? Of course, he will be furious now that I have gone and done so and perturbed beyond measure that he will have to deal with the children. But it seems fair after all I have suffered for him. He can pick up the pieces and carry on with his children from here. I am looking forward to some rest and a freeing of my mind from the constant demands of figuring out how to avenge my family. You have no idea how exhausting is the heavy burden of revenge.

"And that is my story, ladies. You may applaud . . . or not, but I for one could not be prouder. For it takes bravery and great courage to sustain righteous indignation."

No one moved, no one spoke as Chief Inspector Lewis, Constable Claerk, and Granda came out from the back room. Lewis quickly moved behind Eva and told her to stand.

"Eva Gallagher Archer, you are being arrested and taken into custody for the murder of Eireann Swan." Eva stood tall, her head erect and shoulders back as she looked straight ahead, and offered no resistance as she was led away to the waiting police car.

Drew and her grandfather followed the officers out the door and watched as Eva was gently helped into the car. Drew caught a view of the woman in the rear seat as the vehicle pulled slowly away from the library. She looked annoyed now, as though this was all a great inconvenience.

Drew went back into the library where the women were putting the room back to rights. They moved in silence. Charlotte and Lillian cleared the tables as Nonna, Serena, and Joanne moved the furniture into place. Sitting down at a small side table, Drew made notes in her journal as the women busied about her. She then gathered up her coat and satchel and bade them all thank you and goodbye. Walking to the promenade, heavy in thought and weary to her core, she felt awash in sadness. Her fatigue had her wishing she was headed toward her bed rather than walking toward the tall young man she saw in the distance.

Liam was leaning against the ornate balustrade that lined the long pier, looking out over the water. She would tell him of Eva's confession and lack of remorse over Eireann's death, of the triumph of revenge burning hot in the woman's soul.

As Chief Inspector Lewis escorted Eva to the waiting patrol car, Drew had caught his arm and asked about the children.

"Don't concern yourself, Miss Davies. Mr. Archer is with them, and we will be questioning him shortly about what he did or did not know regarding his wife's actions. We will have a woman officer with the children during that time."

But that was far from true. The reality in Drew's mind was the truth that two children had been abandoned by their mother's desperate quest to atone for her father's and brother's deaths. Her children would forever suffer the consequences of their mother's crime—suffer in ways large and small. Would Eva ever come to realize that revenge culminating in murder is never worth the cost of the fallout?

Liam turned around and saw Drew drawing near, tears lining her face. She fell into his arms, leaning into a safe haven of comfort.

After several minutes, she eased back against the balustrade and looked into his deep blue eyes. "Eva Archer confessed to murdering Eireann. I am so sorry, Liam," she said, choking now on her tears. "Now we know the how and the why, but it doesn't make it any better. You have my deepest sympathy."

Liam's attempts to blink away his own tears proved futile. Drew pulled out the handkerchief from her pocket and dabbed them away. He cleared his throat before saying, "But knowing will provide us with closure, and that will help ease the pain. I will ring Auntie Theda when I get home. I know she will be relieved as well. What a difficult day you have had, Drew. How amazing it is that you were able to deduce that it was Eva Archer. How did you do that?"

"I didn't know for sure it was her, but we needed to begin eliminating suspects. She definitely had motive, opportunity, and means—and my intuition told me to begin with her."

After some silence, and deep breaths, she asked, "Now, tell me about your day, filled with weddings, funerals, and baptisms."

Liam smiled and relaxed perceptibly. "The wedding was beautiful, the funeral was well-attended, and the baptisms were a blessing and the best part of my day.

"I once read a quote by the Indian poet, Rabindranath Tagore. He said,

'Every child comes with the message that God is not yet discouraged of man.' I think of that every time I hold a wee babe and bless them into the world. I know that that blessing is truth, because with each baptism, I hold hope in my arms."

"Hope. I always believe hope to be the most important of all virtues. My hope for this moment is that the Archer children find people to love and nurture them and that they can sustain hope for their future."

"And my hope for this moment, Drew Davies, is that tomorrow will find us both, and all those we love and care about, filled with gratitude. There is much to be thankful for."

Drew could only nod as she quietly laid her head upon his shoulder and his arms folded around her. After a few moments, they said goodnight. She convinced him she wanted to walk home on her own and would be fine. And she was not alone, but accompanied by her swirling emotions and thoughts on this eventful day, longing for her family.

LOOSE ENDS – MONDAY, APRIL 21

At eight o'clock the next morning, Drew and Howard were both working at their desks when the police rang. They were both being summoned to meet with Chief Inspector Lewis at eleven. Granda assured the officer on the phone that they would be there. Upon arrival at the police station, they were silently escorted into the chief's office and told to take seats, that the chief inspector would be with them soon.

"It feels like we're in trouble. What do you think the chief has to say to us?" asked Drew.

"I believe it's just routine, going over what happened at the library yesterday and wrapping up loose ends. But I do expect he will have something to say about the less-than-conventional method of securing Mrs. Archer's confession."

With no acknowledgment or greeting for the two people seated in his office, Chief Inspector Lewis opened the door, walked around to his desk, sat down, put on his glasses, and opened a file. He sat in silence for some moments before looking up at them. "Thank you for coming in today. We need to go over all that occurred at the library yesterday, and let's begin with answers to some questions.

"Why was I not informed of this plan, this library tea, before it took place?"

Drew took a deep breath and began. "I knew, after learning about her family's deaths in the IRA bombings, that Mrs. Archer had motive and opportunity for Miss Swan's murder. But I had no way of knowing if she would confess once she was confronted with evidence of how the murder was carried out. The tea could have been just that, a spring tea at the library and nothing else. Especially after Joanne heard Rex and Eileen's conversation in the park. And remember, Chief Inspector, I did ring and give you that information first thing the next morning."

Howard added, "And I also rang you the morning of the tea, filling you in, Lewis, and asking for your presence should there be a scuffle or at best a confession."

"Ringing me just a few hours before the event says to me that you didn't want the authorities to know in advance because you, Miss Davies, were hell-bent on carrying out your plan rather than letting us do our jobs. You were placing yourselves and all the women at the library in possible danger."

"I can see how that might look, Chief Inspector Lewis, but I knew you were there listening from the back room, and should anything happen, you would take charge. And that is exactly what you did when you arrested Mrs. Archer. I merely presented the woman with an opportunity to tell her story, which ended in a confession."

"You are very convincing, Miss Davies, but while we are all relieved the murder has been solved, I cannot condone your unorthodox methods. Do you understand?"

"Yes, sir, I understand."

The chief leaned back in his chair, removed his spectacles, and said, "And this isn't the first time, Miss Davies, that you have inserted yourself into a murder investigation and put yourself in danger. I would like to have your assurance, and yours as well, Howard, that from here on out you will both stay away from murder and police business. Do I have your assurances?"

"But, sir, I hope you realize that I never intentionally go looking for murder and—"

"Miss Davies, I don't want to hear any explanations or anything else from you other than you will mind your own business. Do I make myself clear?"

"Yes, sir. Perfectly," said Drew.

Howard nodded at the chief inspector.

"Alright, get on with your day. And I hope the next time I see you both it is under more pleasant circumstances."

Drew and Granda rose from their seats. Chief Inspector Lewis walked around his desk and, before opening the door, said, "And how about that pint we keep saying we'll drink together, Howard? Next Friday at the pub?"

"I look forward to it," said Howard as he and the chief shook hands.

"And, Miss Davies," said Chief Inspector Lewis as he extended his hand for her to shake, "I do commend you for your keen mind and determination, but again, I strongly suggest you turn it toward less dangerous pursuits."

"Speaking of pursuing information, Chief Inspector, I assume you questioned Rex and Eileen after I rang you Friday morning. What did they tell you when confronted with knowledge of their conversation in the park?

"Not that I need to relay that information to you, Miss Davies, but since you brought the information forward, I'll explain. Although what they were discussing at that time sounded very suspicious and could be construed as having to do with the murder, they were actually ending an affair of several months with one another. It seems Eva Archer had recently had a fling with an actor in London, and Rex decided it was tit for tat, so to speak. That was the revenge that Eileen Bennett was referring to."

It was not until they were both back in the lorry that Drew said, "Well, that was interesting. I don't know whether to feel chastised or congratulated. Maybe a little of both. And there are still loose ends, such as did Eileen Bennett secure the poison for Eva? Was William Bennet in any way involved? And most of all, was Eireann Swan truly responsible for the deaths of Eva's family and or Eileen's mother? She was never arrested or brought to trial for murder, but I can better understand why Eva and Eileen are so bitter. I really do hate loose ends."

"And we'll never know, Drew Girl, if there was a cast of accomplices on that train. Nor will we ever know if Eireann Swan actually activated the lethal explosion that resulted in so many people losing their lives. Murder is always heinous and, in my opinion, never justified."

The two of them sat some time in silent reflection before Granda said, "Lewis was just doing his job in calling us in today. If you must know, my sentiments are the same as the chief's. While I agree that you have a detective's keen and curious mind, it is hard for me to see you in harm's way. Turning your attentions to something other than solving murders would go a long way in making my life and your nonna's less stressful."

"Well, hopefully I'll hear that the van guard job is mine, and that will certainly give me something new to focus on. Have you heard anything yet?"

"Ie, I have Drew Girl, but it isn't what you want to hear."

"The job isn't to be mine, is it? Who did they give it to? Please don't say it was Jonesy's nephew, anyone but him."

"I'm sorry but yes, the job was given to Michael Jones. It was to be expected, a young man returning from the war looking for work and Jonesy, his railroading uncle, putting a relative forward for the position."

"An advantage over a more qualified woman, you mean, and an applicant currently employed by the railway and also from a railroading family. I knew it was improbable that I would get the job, but it was so logical since I was the more experienced person as well as completely qualified."

Drew sat up straighter in the seat of the lorry and turned to look out the window. "The unfairness of it all just makes me so angry. And embarrassed. I have no reason to be embarrassed, but it will be hard to show up back at the station with everyone knowing I was passed over unfairly."

"The unfortunate truth is that no one will see the decision as unfair except you and me. Rather, it was what was expected. Words will not make you feel any better, but I am proud of you for your tenacity, your intelligence, and your grit in applying for the job. You are a strong woman, and maybe it's time to think about other opportunities."

"I love trains, the railways, and everything about them, but I am realistic enough to know that there is no way forward for me working in any other capacity other than in an office where there is no challenge, no adventure, and no feeling of accomplishment in the days' same routines. What am I going to do?"

"Right now, today, we are going to drive back to the station and continue doing our jobs, which are very important to the running of the station and the railway. You'll get through the next days and feelings of disappointment and frustration, and as you do, you'll begin to consider different jobs that might provide you with challenges. Think on that, my Drew Girl."

"I have thought on that most of my life, and being a railway woman is who I am and what I am meant to do. You know as well as I do, I am third generation—it's in our blood."

Granda merely nodded his head in understanding, started the lorry, and headed back to the station with a strong-minded and determined railroader seated beside him. He had a few ideas of his own for what she might do, but he needed to do some thinking on it and Drew needed time.

EPILOGUE

Liam Leaving – Tuesday, April 22

Liam stood beside the train, hat in hand, his portmanteau beside him on the platform. He purposely did not tell his congregation when his train would be leaving. It was better for many reasons.

Drew stepped from the station's wide doors out to where the pulsing train sat billowing steam in preparation for departure. Looking left, she saw Liam standing in solitude beside the waiting carriage. She alone knew he was leaving on this early morning train.

She had spent a sleepless night thinking on all that had happened over the last weeks. Masking her feelings of hopelessness lest he see her so unsettled, she calmly measured her steps as she walked toward the man. Her greatest desire was to run to him, asking him to stay. Never would she do that but rather would send him off with dry eyes and a heavy heart.

Liam watched her approaching. As they grew closer, he opened his arms. It was like leaning into love.

"I'll tend the house and your gardens, Liam O'Neill," Drew said quietly in his ear.

He gently moved them apart and looked down into the eyes of the young woman who had become so important to him. "*Our* gardens, Drew Davies, and they will become as lovely as you."

"Oh, Liam."

"I know, Drew."

With a sad smile and a gentle hand to her cheek, he turned and boarded the train, never looking back as he moved into the carriage, away from possibility.

He wondered, not for the first time, if he were making a terrible mistake.

READER'S GUIDE

1. Imagine the center of your community devastated by multiple nights of bombing, and much of the infrastructure of your life and the lives of those around you is destroyed. After the bombing has stopped, what are the first three things you would do and why? Consider a natural disaster. Think: earthquake, hurricane, flooding, landslide, extreme heat wave, freezing temps with no electricity, etc. Do you have an emergency pack ready in case of a disaster? Have you ever lived through such an experience?

2. Was there a time in your life when you experienced disappointment that brought you low? A broken heart, a job or career that didn't work out, the loss of loved ones. How did you handle your disappointment, and how did life move on for you?

3. Love is a precarious conundrum—a roller coaster of emotional highs and lows. Have you experienced that roller coaster in your own life? Have you ever found yourself attracted to more than one person at the same time? What did you do?

4. If you were Drew, and you being you, who would you be most attracted to, Sam or Liam, and why? Which man do you think Drew would be happiest with and why?

5. Like my Grandmother Edith, I love to garden, cook, read, and write stories. Drew and Nonna also share many of the same interests. What similar interests do you share with your mother or grandmother(s)?

6. Every generation is the living embodiment of history during their lifetime. Is there another time in history that you would have liked to experience and why?

7. In this unsettled world of ours, what are two things you might begin doing today that would contribute to a better world? Why have you chosen what you did?

HISTORICAL PERSPECTIVES

RATIONING

Rationing of the basic necessities of life, including food, clothing, and fuel, is a consequence of war. In the United Kingdom, rationing began in September 1939.

Fuel, because it was needed by the military, was rationed first. After priority was accorded to the military, petrol was allotted to emergency services, bus companies, and farmers. It was dyed red to prohibit its illegal use and became known as "red diesel." Fines and jail sentences were doled out if you were found using the red fuel.

Bacon, butter, and sugar were rationed next, followed closely by all meat products, tea, biscuits, cereals, cheese, eggs, flour, lard, milk, and canned and dried fruit. All items were rationed by weight except meat, which was allotted by fixed price.

Bread, considered an important food staple, was rationed from June 1946 to July 1948 and became known as "the national loaf." Its mushy gray consistency was blamed for a myriad of intestinal ailments. Other than watered-down beer, alcohol was scarce, since distillers were all off fighting the war, and the importation of barley was nil. But beer was also considered a "vital food stuff" and a morale booster, so even the diluted version was never rationed.

Fish were not rationed; however, commercial fishing vessels were requisitioned by the military, leaving only small boats for fishing and shipping. Supplies of fish to the public decreased to 30% of pre-war availability. When fish and chips were available, they were considered to be substandard due to the poor quality of the cooking oil.

The many constraints of rationing created a climate of frustrated creativity for homemakers attempting to feed their families meals that would be nutritious and appear appetizing. Obtaining the foodstuffs was a daunting task, requiring long waits in ration lines outside of stores and markets that often ran out of what you hoped to secure that day. If you were not there early enough, or the store ran out before your turn, you went home with one less item—or two or three—to feed your family. The many shops and markets had different items available on different days of the week, making shopping an arduous task that required patience, organization, and a considerable amount of one's time.

The British Ministry of Food printed flyers and leaflets to help housewives create recipes and also to bolster their spirits. Radio programs on food preparation attempted to do the same, and neighboring women traded tips and recipes. Fascinating books have been written about the subject of "mend and make do" during those times of shortages. Two books I found very interesting, humorous, and enlightening are *Spuds, Spam and Eating for Victory* by Katherine Knight and the very informative and entertaining novel, *The Kitchen Front* by Jennifer Ryan.

Rationing did not completely end in Britain until July 1954. Some studies indicate that all available food was distributed equally to everyone, and so, since the diet contained enough vitamins and nutrients to sustain adequate nutrition, infant mortality decreased and life expectancy increased, excluding the loss of life due to conflict. (Of course that was never completely true, as the black market supplied additional stuffs to the wealthy and the conniving.) While the studies may hold some truth, there is no disputing that rationing was a severe hardship, just one more that caused emotional and physical distress to civilians, adding to the futility and chaos of war.

RECONSTRUCTION

The books in the Drew Davies Railway Mysteries are historical cozy mysteries with some spice of romance sprinkled throughout. The settings are always in Southern Wales, in the town of Swansea and the village of Mumbles following World War II.

Through the day-to-day lives of my characters, there are descriptions of the post-war circumstances of their lives. However, I do not specifically address the harrowing years of reconstruction and the economic, social, political, and psychological repercussions of rebuilding lives literally from the ashes of destruction.

People were focused on survival. Homes were lost in the bombings, and they struggled to find places to live. Factories and places of employment were destroyed, and jobs were difficult to find. In many instances, post-war reconstruction did not begin until sometimes decades after the various peace accords were signed. Food rationing in Britain continued for fifteen long years.

The systems of local government were fractured and dysfunctional, mired in confusion, lack of funding, and disorganization. It was a time of chaos across Western and Eastern Europe. The Allied powers, United Nations, and the International Committee of the Red Cross assisted greatly. The Marshall Plan was passed by the US Congress in 1948 and funneled $13.3 billion over the next four years to aid in European reconstruction efforts.

Cities and towns at the local level, however, were expected to assist in the rebuilding efforts, but because there was no work, no funding, and little infrastructure to organize and rebuild, these places lay in ruins for many years, sometimes decades, before resources were in place to begin construction.

Swansea, Wales, one of the settings in these books, suffered three nights of the German blitz. During the attack, 1,273 high-explosive bombs and 56,000 incendiary bombs were dropped over the city center. The piers and docks of the city were the Germans' intended targets, but calculations went awry. Two hundred and thirty people were killed, 409 injured and 7,000 citizens lost their homes. Reconstruction efforts lagged due to what I have discussed above: lack of funds and workers, organization, politics, etc. It wasn't until the 1970s that reconstruction efforts in Swansea began and are ongoing today.

Unfortunately, social and emotional recovery from the atrocities of World War II will never fully be healed, but the lessons learned hopefully will cause humanity to consider the unspeakable cost of war and its profound repercussions. History must be truthfully taught and understood, as it often portends the future.

ACKNOWLEDGMENTS

Writing historical fiction and conducting the necessary research to ground the story provides the writer the gift of meeting new people and making new friends. And when these new friends, such as John and Carol Powell of Mumbles, Wales, welcome you to their beautiful village and show you all the sites you are writing about, it is a magical adventure. Thank you, John and Carol, for taking us to those places in Mumbles and Swansea that brought my characters and settings to life. What amazing historians you are and what marvelous companions as we shared those days of exploring together. And thank you, as well, for always reading my drafts and imparting wonderful insights for revisions and additions. I am forever grateful.

My first book, *The Lavender House in Meuse*, went to press in 2014. Ten years later and with the completion of this fifth book, many of the same wonderful people remain as my support team. Those include daughters Laura and Taya, readers of my first drafts, who always provide insight and direction, and my husband, Terry, my biggest cheerleader, who makes me smile as he tells me whatever he is reading is the best I have ever done. Thank you all!

My dear friend Dominique Dailly continues to read the final edited drafts, always providing me honest feedback through her eyes as a thoughtful, prolific, and intelligent reader. Our Friday lunches are always full of laughter, discussion, talk of this and that—and sometimes my books. Thank you, Dominique.

Isn't the cover of the book you are holding beautiful?! When I returned from Wales and was thinking about the vision for this book, I knew I wanted it to portray the beautifully expansive boardwalk at the Mumbles pier. My talented sister, Kathleen Noble, paints all the pictures for all my covers, and I was excited to share my thoughts for the front of this book. She told me to send her a sketch, which is like asking me to draw a straight line (impossible), but I always try, as she always asks. When I sent her the sketch, she called, and we had a good laugh over my very poor drawing ability. Then we talked about the vision for the book I knew she could create and which she did. Thank you, as always, Kathy. This exceptionally talented sister of mine is an award-winning artist, and you can see all her work at kanobleartist.com.

Have you heard me mention Editor Extraordinaire, Sally Carr? Yes, I am sure you have, as she has been with me from the beginning and who I hope will be there when I finish the last word of my last book, somewhere in the future. Thank you, Sally, for always embracing my stories, my characters, and my vision. Your excellent editing makes the books the best they can be and I am always so grateful.

And you, Dear Readers of my books, thank you for finding these stories and letting me know how enjoyable they are to you. You inspire my writing, and I truly aspire to continue to bring you historical fiction that you find enlightening and entertaining. Please keep in touch, as I always appreciate your emails and comments on my website.

Gnoble_sanderson@comcast.net
Gailnoblesanderson.com